**Welcome to the world
of Sydney Harbour Hospital**

**(or *SHH*… for short—
because secrets never stay hidden for long!)**

Looking out over cosmopolitan Sydney Harbour, Australia's premier teaching hospital is a hive of round-the-clock activity—with a *very* active hospital grapevine.

With the most renowned (and gorgeous!) doctors in Sydney working side by side, professional and sensual tensions run sky-high—there's *always* plenty of romantic rumours to gossip about…

*Who's been kissing who in the on-call room? What's going on between legendary heart surgeon Finn Kennedy and tough-talking A&E doctor Evie Lockheart? And what's wrong with Finn?*

Find out in this enthralling new eight-book continuity from Medical™ Romance—indulge yourself with eight helpings of romance, emotion and gripping medical drama!

**Sydney Harbour Hospital**
***From saving lives to sizzling seduction,
these doctors are the very best!***

**Dear Reader**

When I was asked to write for the *Sydney Harbour Hospital* series I was blown away with excitement. In my non-biased (?) opinion Sydney is the most beautiful city in the world, and Sydney Harbour Hospital is the most awesome hospital. Let's face it: it's been created by eight great Aussie authors, so what's not to love? Our city's fantastic, our staff are fantastic, and the drama, heartache, laughter, gossip and sheer love of life engendered by the staff of SHH will suck you in as it's sucked me in. I loved it from the moment I read the outline. This series will catch your heartstrings like no other. Oh, and did I mention I think it's good?

I adore the charismatic Dr Finn Kennedy, whose story weaves through the whole series, but most of all I love my Luke and my Lily. I hope they tug at your heartstrings as much as they tugged on mine.

Happy reading

*Marion Lennox*

# SYDNEY HARBOUR HOSPITAL: LILY'S SCANDAL

BY
MARION LENNOX

First published in Great Britain 2012
by Mills & Boon, an imprint of Harlequin (UK) Limited.
Large Print edition 2012
Harlequin (UK) Limited, Eton House,
18-24 Paradise Road, Richmond, Surrey TW9 1SR

© Harlequin Books S.A. 2012

Special thanks and acknowledgement are given
to Marion Lennox for her contribution to the
*Sydney Harbour Hospital* series

ISBN: 978 0 263 22464 1

**Marion Lennox** is a country girl, born on an Australian dairy farm. She moved on—mostly because the cows just weren't interested in her stories! Married to a 'very special doctor', Marion writes Medical™ Romances, as well as Mills & Boon® Romances. (She used a different name for each category for a while—if you're looking for her past Mills & Boon Romances, search for author Trisha David as well.) She's now had 75 romance novels accepted for publication.

In her non-writing life Marion cares for kids, cats, dogs, chooks and goldfish. She travels, she fights her rampant garden (she's losing) and her house dust (she's lost). Having spun in circles for the first part of her life, she's now stepped back from her 'other' career, which was teaching statistics at her local university. Finally she's reprioritised her life, figured out what's important, and discovered the joys of deep baths, romance and chocolate. Preferably all at the same time!

**Recent titles by the same author:**

DYNAMITE DOC OR CHRISTMAS DAD?*
THE DOCTOR AND THE RUNAWAY HEIRESS*
NIKKI AND THE LONE WOLF**
MARDIE AND THE CITY SURGEON**

*Mills & Boon® Medical™ Romance
**Mills & Boon® Romance *Banksia Bay* miniseries

**These books are also available in ebook format from www.millsandboon.co.uk**

**Sydney Harbour Hospital**

*Sexy surgeons, dedicated doctors,*
*scandalous secrets, on-call dramas…*

**Welcome to the world of Sydney Harbour Hospital**
**(or *SHH*… for short—**
**because secrets never stay hidden for long!)**

This month enjoy our fantastic medical duo as
new nurse Lily gets caught up in the hot-bed of hospital gossip in
**SYDNEY HARBOUR HOSPITAL: LILY'S SCANDAL**
**by Marion Lennox**

Then gorgeous paediatrician Teo
comes to single mum Zoe's rescue in
**SYDNEY HARBOUR HOSPITAL: ZOE'S BABY**
**by Alison Roberts**

Don't miss sexy Sicilian playboy Luca
as he finally meets his match this March
**SYDNEY HARBOUR HOSPITAL: LUCA'S BAD GIRL**
**by Amy Andrews**

Then in April Hayley opens Tom's eyes to love in
**SYDNEY HARBOUR HOSPITAL: TOM'S REDEMPTION**
**by Fiona Lowe**

Join heiress Lexi as she learns to put the past behind her in May…
**SYDNEY HARBOUR HOSPITAL: LEXI'S SECRET**
**by Melanie Milburne**

In June adventurer Charlie helps shy Bella fulfil her dreams—
and find love on the way!
**SYDNEY HARBOUR HOSPITAL: BELLA'S WISHLIST**
**by Emily Forbes**

Then single mum Emily gives no-strings-attached surgeon Marco
a reason to stay in
**SYDNEY HARBOUR HOSPITAL: MARCO'S TEMPTATION**
**by Fiona McArthur**

And finally join us in August as Ava and James
realise their marriage really is worth saving in
**SYDNEY HARBOUR HOSPITAL: AVA'S RE-AWAKENING**
**by Carol Marinelli**

And not forgetting Sydney Harbour Hospital's legendary heart
surgeon Finn Kennedy. This brooding maverick keeps his women
on hospital rotation… But can new doc Evie Lockheart unlock the
secrets to his guarded heart? Find out in this enthralling new
eight-book continuity from Medical™ Romance.

A collection impossible to resist!

**These books are also available in ebook format**
**from www.millsandboon.co.uk**

# CHAPTER ONE

LUKE WILLIAMS had been operating since dawn. All he wanted was bed. Instead he was coping with stinking tallow, teenage hysteria and the director of surgery and the representative of the founders of this hospital thinking pistols at dawn.

'You said multiple burns. Four children. I've spent most of the night with a kid with a collapsed lung, and you wake me for this…'

Luke's boss, Finn Kennedy, the taciturn head of surgery at Sydney Harbour Hospital, was practically rigid with fury, but Dr Evie Lockheart, emergency physician, was giving it right back.

'I was told four children fell into a vat of boiling tallow from the meatworks. You think that's not worth getting you and Luke down here? I wanted the best.'

'Luke has other things to do as well. Like sleeping. And boiling? It must have been barely warm. You should have checked.'

'And waste precious time? Pull your head in, Kennedy.'

Luke sucked his breath in at that. These guys were powerhouses in this hospital. Evie Lockheart, of Endowing-the-Hospital-with-Serious-Money Lockheart fame, and Finn Kennedy, the Do-Not-Cross Director of Surgery, had personalities to match their egos. Powerful intellects, serious commitment, serious…conflict. Conflict getting worse.

Could he back away?

No.

School holidays. A meat-processing operation out in the suburbs, with inadequate security. Four teenaged boys, fifteen or sixteen, egging each other to walk the plank—on rollerblades!—over a two-thousand-gallon vat of tallow being rendered down.

They were lucky the heat had only just been turned on. They'd fallen into the equivalent of a bath that was a bit too hot.

Through the office window, the kids and their frightened parents looked a pool of misery. The stench was unbelievable, but it could have been much worse. A pert little blonde nurse was swabbing tallow from one kid's legs, exposing only minor scalding.

He couldn't leave, he decided, not until things had

calmed down. Meanwhile he had a choice. Join in the fight. Look at the kids. Look at the nurse.

This was a no-brainer.

The woman was cute, he thought, even in her ER scrubs. Her blonde curls were wisping from under her cap. As he watched, she tucked them back in, and then glanced through the window.

He caught her gaze and saw laughter, quickly suppressed.

She'd be seeing the conflict, he thought, even if she couldn't hear it. Was she laughing at these two? Not a good idea, he told her silently. Laughter would be really unwise right now, even for him, and he'd been working here for nearly ten years. He fought—quite hard—the urge to smile back.

He also fought the urge to hold his nose. This stink was permeating the whole floor.

'The gastro outbreak has given us nursing shortages through the whole hospital,' Evie was snapping. 'I didn't have the nursing staff to clean and check each of these boys before calling you. Possible burns, possible major trauma, it's my job to call for back-up.'

'They're not traumatised,' Finn snapped back.

But they were, Luke conceded, looking through at the very-sorry-for-themselves kids. It looked to him like their parents had initially been terrified and then expressed shock in the form of anger. He'd seen it time and time again in this job, fright finding vent in fury.

A couple of the kids had been crying. Tough teenage boys, scalded and scared… They should do a bit of reassuring.

But first he needed to defuse the battle of the Titans. How to stop World War III without accidentally escalating it?

'You think your power gives you the right…' Finn Williams was growling to the Lockheart heiress.

Luke gave an inward groan and thought, Here we go.

The little blonde nurse had disappeared into the storeroom. Good idea, he thought. Could he follow?

Not so much. Finn was his direct boss. Evie was the granddaughter of the founder of this place.

If he valued his job he needed to stick around while these power-mongers tore each other's throats out.

In truth he wasn't so worried about his job. As head of the plastic surgery team at the Harbour his credentials made him pretty much unsackable. But as well as being his boss, Finn was also his friend, or as much of a friend as either of them wanted. The last few weeks, he'd watched Finn's perennially short fuse grow even shorter.

Finn and Evie had sparked off each other from the moment they'd met. As a junior doctor, Evie had dared query one of Finn's decisions. She'd been wrong, she'd apologised, but Finn had mocked her family's right to power, and their relationship had been...*interesting* ever since. But now, even for Finn, his anger was over the top.

It was messing with staff morale. It was also worrying, and Luke didn't like being worried. Luke Williams was a man who held himself apart. He didn't get close to people.

He was worrying now about his friend.

And through the window...

He hadn't seen this nurse before.

Pretty. Great eyes. They were a blue that made you feel like diving into clear, sunlit water on a hot day. It must be her first night on the job, he decided. He would have noticed those eyes.

Where was she?

Maybe she'd gone to get a hose.

'There may well be second- or third-degree burns under that mess,' Evie was saying, almost hissing her anger.

'There's no sign of shock. All they need is a good wash.'

'And then assessment,' Evie snapped. 'So then I'll call you back?'

'You won't need to call us back. I'm guessing first-degree burns at worst.'

'Could we find out?

It was Blue Eyes, out of the storeroom, popping into their private war with her arms full of plastic. 'Sorry,' she said, blithely, as if she hadn't noticed any anger. 'I know it's not my place but I've spent the last couple of years working in a country hospital where all staff step in at need. I'm thinking we have four kids here, and four medics if you count me. How about we all put on protective gear, get each of these guys in a shower cubicle and do an individual check for any burn that needs attention? Split up the work from there.'

Whoa. Luke's jaw practically hit his ankles. Did she know who she had here? Only three of Sydney Harbour Hospital's most influential doctors. Head of Surgery. Head of Plastics. Member of the Lockheart family.

She wasn't wearing the Harbour uniform. *She was an agency nurse?*

She was holding out the protective gear as if she was expecting them to take it.

But… What choice did they have? There were no nurses spare. The gastro outbreak had badly affected the hospital, plus there'd been a brawl early in the night; he'd seen it on his way off duty. Drunk casualties. That meant intensive nursing, guys who'd been stitched up but who were still affected by alcohol.

So Evie had been left with one lone nurse and four filthy kids with possible burns. An emergency department full of hysterical patients, parents and stink. No wonder she'd called for help, even if she'd called for help a bit high up the food chain.

Maybe the nurse was right, this was the fastest solution. And, besides, those eyes…

'I'll take the beefy one with the scowl,' he said, taking a set of waterproof gear.

Evie gazed at him, speechless. 'You…'

'You called me,' he said mildly. 'I assume you need me.' He grabbed another waterproof set and tossed it to Finn. 'It'll do us good,' he said. 'Bit of stress release. You want to take the little guy with freckles?'

Finn caught the waterproofs. Looked flabbergasted.

'I'll do the skinny one,' Blue Eyes said, and handed the last set of overalls to Evie.

There was a moment's pregnant pause. Very pregnant.

Blue Eyes calmly hauled on her waterproofs, then bent and started putting on boots.

She had wispy blonde curls on the back of her neck, Luke thought. Cute. Really cute.

Was that the reason he hauled on boots as well?

No. This was sensible. He didn't succumb to testosterone when it came to cute, not any more, but this place was clogged with stinking kids. They all needed checking, there were no nurses free and this way... Blue Eyes had it right, in the time they spent arguing they could get them checked and out of here.

'I'll ring the cleaning staff and tell them we need this place cleared while we're showering,' Blue Eyes said, now clad all in waterproofs. She tugged open the door, allowing contact between doctors and patients. *Before she even had Finn's okay.*

'Ross, you go with Dr Williams, Robbie, you're with Dr Lockheart, Craig, you're with Mr Kennedy and, Jason, you're with me,' she said. She turned to the parents. 'Could you leave the kids with us? They're in the best of hands; we have the most senior doctors in the hospital working with them. We'll clean them, check there are no problem burns and then get them back to you. Maybe you could find an all-night supermarket and pick up some loose clothes. Is that okay with everyone?'

But before they could answer they were interrupted. 'Excuse me...' The night receptionist edged into the emergency area like a scared rabbit. Of course she was nervous, Luke thought. Everyone in this hospital was nervous around Finn Kennedy, and for good reason. 'The police are here,' she ventured, and before she could say more two cops pushed past her.

Uh-oh. They hadn't realised, Luke thought with grim humour, that they'd just entered Finn Kennedy territory. Facing gun-toting drug dealers might be safer.

'These youths are facing charges of breaking and entering,' the older policeman said, looking at the boys as if they were truly bad smells. 'The orderly outside said they don't seem badly injured. Can we get the paperwork out of the way so we can get on with our night's work?'

Uh-oh, indeed. Luke held his breath. Finn's fuse, already short, was suddenly down to the core explosive, and he had a target.

'Breaking and entering?' His voice was icy.

'That's right, sir.' The cop still didn't see the danger—but here it came.

'These kids have fallen into exposed hot fat,' Finn snarled. 'A life-threatening hazard to anyone who comes near it. An unsecured environment. Unlocked windows. You know as well as I do that a simple padlock on a closed door doesn't begin to cover such a risk. Breaking and entering… You can tell whoever's thinking of pressing charges that he can go back to whatever stinking wormhole he crawled from and expect a visit from Occupational Health and Safety, with lawyers following. These children are traumatised enough, and you're adding more. Now get out of this hospital before I phone someone with enough clout to have you thrown out.'

Then, as the cops backed out with astonishing speed, he turned to Luke. 'What are you waiting for? Get those waterproofs on and get these kids clean. Do what the nurse says. Now.'

The really good thing about being a nobody was that it didn't matter whose toes you stood on. You were still just a nobody.

These guys were all big-wigs. Lily knew it, but she'd watched the outburst of sound and fury with dispassion, not really fussed if the anger turned on her. What was the worst that could happen? She'd move on.

There were other hospitals. Her credentials were good. She could go somewhere else and be anonymous all over again.

The feeling was extraordinary. She felt like she was floating, light and free. She'd escaped.

She'd return eventually to Lighthouse Cove, the tiny community that judged her mother and who judged her. She knew deep down that this was a momentary escape. A promise was a promise. But right now her mother was in the middle of a dizzying affair with the local parish vicar, the whole town was on fire with gossip and Lily was staying right here, in nice, anonymous Sydney.

She was a bank nurse, employed by an agency. She was sent where she was needed, so if she stood on toes, if she wasn't needed, if these Very Important Doctors decided they wished to dispense with her services, then so be it.

She practically chuckled as she led Jason into a shower cubicle and along the line of cubicles three Very Important Doctors followed her lead.

Two of them looked grim. The other...not so much. He was the head of plastic surgery, she gathered. Luke Williams looked lean and ripped, hovering above six feet, with sun-bleached brown hair and deep green eyes that glinted with repressed laughter. Very repressed, though. She caught his gaze and she could have sworn he was laughing, but he averted his eyes fast. It wouldn't do to laugh out loud.

There wasn't enough laughter in her life, she thought, and she needed it. But she'd taken the first step, and it had felt good to exchange her first attempt at laughter in her new job with a doctor as hunky as Luke Williams.

There's an inappropriate thought, she chided herself, but she was still smiling inwardly.

'Will this hurt?' Jason quavered, and she gave him a reassuring smile.

'I suspect mostly just your pride. We need to get those clothes off. Are you hurting?'

'Stinging,' he admitted. 'A bit.'

The meatworks proprietor should have washed them straight away, Lily thought, growing serious. If the tallow had been really hot, they'd have been facing a nightmare. The owner of the meatworks hadn't checked. He'd simply threatened them with police and they'd fled. Their parents had brought them straight here, with hot tallow still intact. If it had been boiling it would have kept right on burning.

They'd been so lucky. Apparently the vat had only just started warming. The boys had climbed in through a high window, seen huge planks laid across to skim off impurities and dared each other to rollerblade across. The stupidity left Lily breathless. She'd heard the outline. One kid falling, clutching his mate as he fell, both grabbing the planking, which had come loose, tumbling their mates in after them.

Lily turned the shower to soft pressure, skin temperature. She put Jason's hands on the rails and produced scissors.

'Just to my knickers,' Jason whimpered.

'There's nothing I haven't seen,' Lily told him. 'If you've burned anything personal, you'll need it fixed.'

Another whimper.

'There's nothing to this,' she told him cheerfully. 'These jeans are going to stink for ever so we might as well cut 'em off. So…rollerblading over steaming tallow. Quite a trick. How long have you been blading?'

'A…a year.' The water was streaming over the kid; his clothes were falling away and so was the muck that was covering him.

'You any good?'

'Y-yeah.'

'So of the four of you, who does the neatest tricks?'

Luke was in the next cubicle. He was scissoring clothes from his own kid. Ross had been blustering when Luke had first seen him, whinging to his parents that it wasn't his fault, that his 'expletive' mates had pressured him to do it, Craig had pushed him, his dad should sue.

Under the water, with Luke scissoring off his clothes, he calmed down. His legs were scalded. They were only first-degree burns, though, Luke thought, little worse than sunburn. He'd sting for a week but there'd be little long-term damage.

He'd been swearing as Luke had propelled him under the shower, but when Luke had attacked with scissors…the boy had shut up. 'We need to check down south,' Luke had told him. 'Check everything's still in working order. Steamed balls aren't exactly healthy…' Luke wasn't reassuring him just yet. He liked him quiet, and, besides, with him quiet he could hear the conversation in the next cubicle.

'I've been blading since I was twelve,' Blue Eyes was saying.

'Girls can't blade.' That was her kid—Jason.

'You're kidding me, right? I suspect you'll need to come back in a week or so to make sure these scalds have healed. You bring your blades; I'll organise time off and I'll meet you in the hospital car park. Then we'll see who can't blade.'

Luke blinked. An assignation…

'What, you can blade fast?' Jason had been shakily terrified but Blue Eyes had him distracted. He sounded scornful.

'Fast?' Blue Eyes chuckled, and it was a gorgeous chuckle. 'I do more than fast. I do barrel rolls, grapevines, heel toes, flips, you name it. I'm no gumbie, kiddo.'

'You're kidding.'

'Would I kid about something like blading? My skates were the most important thing in my life for a long, long time.' Blue Eyes suddenly sounded serious. 'It took my mind off other things and I loved it. I can't say I ever bladed over tallow, though.'

'I bet you could.' There was suddenly belief—and admiration—in the kid's voice and Luke found himself agreeing. If this slip of a girl could get Evie and Finn to don waterproofs and wash off tallow, she might be capable of a whole lot more.

He wanted, quite badly, to explore the idea.

Bad idea.

She was an agency nurse. Her uniform told him that. She was one of the casual nurses employed to fill gaps at need in any hospital in the city.

After tonight he might never see her again.

But…she'd made an assignation with Jason in a week. That might mean the agency had positioned her here for more than a night.

She had a great chuckle.

No. Beware of chuckles. And blue eyes. And twinkles.

He thought of Hannah.

He always thought of Hannah. Of course he did. Her memory no longer evoked the searing pain it once had, but instead was a basic part of him, a knowledge that he'd messed with the most precious thing a man could be given. The emotions that went with the sort of involvement he was briefly considering with Blue Eyes were gone. They were left behind in a bleak cemetery with what was left of his wife and his little son.

'Me balls…' Ross whimpered. 'They gunna be okay?'

'They're gunna be fine,' he told the kid he was treating. 'They're a bit pink but they'll live to father sons.'

'I don't want to father kids!' The thought was obviously worse than hot tallow.

'No,' Luke said soothingly. 'I guess you don't, but one day you might. Meanwhile everything's in working order for when you want them to do what they're meant to do. For when your chance in life happens.'

Ross and Jason were sent home. Robbie and Craig were admitted. They'd been in the centre of the vat. It had taken them longer to get out, which meant they had patches of second-degree burning. No full-thickness burns, though. Evie took them in charge, patching them up before admitting them. Luke somehow found himself doing the paperwork while Lily gave Ross and Jason's parents instructions on how to deal with minor scalds.

She then headed off to fill in a police report. Finn might have moved on, but Luke heard Blue Eyes asking questions, getting the boys to sign statements, and he knew because of her the open vats would be covered and there'd be no prosecutions of kids who were just being...kids.

Lily was some nurse.

She wasn't your normal agency nurse. Most agency nurses were looking for a quiet life. They were mums with small kids who worked when they could find someone to care for their children. They were overseas nurses, funding the next adventure. They were older women who worked when grand-kids and aching legs permitted, or they wanted funds for a few retirement treats.

Lily, though, didn't seem to fit any of these cat-egories. She was in her late twenties, he decided, nicely mature. Competent. She had the air of a nurse who'd run her own ward, and who didn't suffer fools gladly. And the way she'd talked to Jason... She didn't sound like a young mum, wearily getting the job done.

He badly needed to get to bed. He had a full list in the morning. He shouldn't be awake now, but first... First he finished the paperwork and casually dropped by Admin. And while he did he just hap-pened to retrieve the fact sheet that had been faxed through with the notification that Blue Eyes had been allocated to work at the Harbour.

Blue Eyes.

Lily Maureen Ellis. Twenty-six years old. Trained at Adelaide. Well trained. He flicked through her list of credentials and blinked—hey, she had plastics experience. She was trained to assist in plastic surgery.

Plus the rest. Intensive care. Paediatrics. Midwifery. He knew the hospital she'd trained in. This woman must be good.

According to the sheet, she'd left Adelaide two years back to run the bush nursing hospital at Lighthouse Cove. He knew Lighthouse Cove. It was a tiny, picturesque town less than an hour's drive from Adelaide.

Fishing, tourists, pubs and not a lot else.

So what had driven Lily Maureen Ellis to pack up and leave Lighthouse Cove and put her name down as an agency nurse in Sydney?

Maybe she was following a man.

Maybe he needed to get some sleep.

'Why the hell aren't you in bed?' It was Finn, scaring the daylights out of him—as normal. The Harbour's Director of Surgery had the tread of a panther—and night sight. Word in the hospital was that there was nothing Finn didn't know. He knew it before it happened.

'Why aren't *you* in bed?' Luke managed back, mildly. 'Have you been giving Evie more grief?'

'I haven't...'

'Yeah, you have,' he said evenly. 'You're tetchy, and you're especially tetchy round Evie. What's eating you?'

'Nothing.'

'Headaches? Sore arm?'

'Why would I have headaches?'

'Beats me,' Luke said mildly. 'But you keep rubbing your head and shoulder, and if anyone puts a foot wrong...'

'Dr Lockheart had no business waking us up,' Finn growled.

'She had four potentially serious burns and one agency nurse. Cut her some slack.'

'She drives me nuts,' Finn said, taking the fact sheet. 'So this is the girl handing out waterproofs.'

'She's got guts.'

'I'm sick of guts,' Finn said. 'Give me a good pliable woman any day. So why are we reading her CV?' He raised an eyebrow in sudden interest. 'Well, well. It's about time...'

'No.'

'No?'

'No.'

'Hannah's been gone for four years now,' Finn said, gentling. 'A man can't mourn for ever.'

'Says the whole hospital,' Luke said grimly. 'It's driving me nuts.'

'So have an affair.' He motioned to the CV. 'Excellent idea. Get them off your back. Get a life.'

'Hannah didn't get a life.'

'It wasn't your fault.'

'So whose fault was it?' he demanded, explosively. 'Fourteen weeks and I didn't even know she was pregnant.'

'You were working seventy hours a week and fronting for exams. Hannah knew the pressures. She was also a nurse and she knew her way around her body. To lock herself in her bedroom and suffer in silence at fourteen weeks pregnant… She was fed up that you were caught up in Theatre. It still smacks of playing the martyr.'

'Don't.'

'Speak ill of the dead? I say it like it is. If one stupid act of martyrdom stops you from getting on with your life…'

'I don't see you getting on with your life.'

Finn stiffened. Finn was his boss, Luke conceded, but their relationship went deeper. He knew as much of Finn's background as anyone did. Finn had a brother who'd been killed in combat. He'd been wounded himself. There'd been a messy relationship with his brother's wife, then a series of forget-the-moment flings.

Was he about to throw those in his boss's face? Maybe not. Not at two in the morning, when they were both sleep deprived—and when a cute little blonde nurse had suddenly appeared in the background behind Finn. Waiting for an opportunity to break in.

'Don't make this about me,' Finn snapped. 'Meanwhile, you...' Finn waved the folder. 'An agency nurse, ripe for the picking. That's what you need. A casual affair and then move on.'

The blue eyes widened.

Luke stifled a groan.

'Excuse me, doctors,' the Agency-Ripe-For-The-Picking nurse said, in a carefully neutral voice. 'The paging system doesn't appear to be working down here. Dr Lockheart has asked me to find you, Dr Williams. Not you, Mr Kennedy. Dr Lockheart's words were, *"Keep that man out of my department at all costs"*. But a child's been admitted with facial injuries from dog bites. Dr Lockheart says to tell you, Dr Williams, that this is serious and could you please come now.'

# CHAPTER TWO

JESSIE BLANDON was headed for Theatre—if he made it that far.

He was four years old. He'd woken in the middle of the night, needing his mother, the bathroom, something. He'd stumbled through the living room. His mother's boyfriend's Rottweiler had been on the couch.

As far as Lily could see, he'd lost half his face. Or not completely lost; it was hanging by a flap. How he'd not bled to death, she didn't know.

Lily didn't have time to think about what she'd just overheard. She flew back to Emergency with Luke.

'Tell me,' he snapped as they strode down the corridor at a pace practised by most emergency medics. Never run in a hospital. Walk—exceedingly fast.

She outlined what she'd seen and Luke's face grew grim.

'Dogs and kids,' he muttered. 'No matter how trustworthy… Hell.'

It was hell. Lily had seen the mother and her boyfriend as the ambulance had wheeled the little boy in. They looked shattered. This would be a great goofy dog, she guessed, normally quiet, startled from sleep into doing what dogs were bred to do. Attack and defend.

How good was this man beside her?

She was about to find out.

She'd not dealt with a case like this at Lighthouse Cove. For the last two years, in her tiny hospital, any serious case had been transferred to Adelaide. Still, she had the training to back her up. Those long years, travelling back and forth from Lighthouse Cove to Adelaide Central, struggling to do her training yet still support her mother, they'd been hard but they'd provided her with skills, so that when Luke Williams said, 'You've done plastics, you trained with Professor Blythe? You'll work with us on this?' she could nod.

But she wasn't nodding with confidence that they'd save the little boy. He was desperately injured. She was only confident that she could back up this man's skills.

If he had the skills.

He did.

To say she was impressed with Luke William's professionalism was an understatement. This was a life-and-death emergency. Every minute they wasted meant this little boy had a smaller chance at life, yet Luke exuded calm from the moment he saw him.

First and foremost he made sure Jessie was feeling no pain. He had an anesthetist there in moments and Jessie was placed swiftly into an induced coma. He assessed what needed to be done. He gave curt, incisive directions with not a word wasted. He even found a moment to talk to the couple outside.

'Things are grim,' he told them. 'There's no way I can assure you your little boy will be okay. I don't know. No one knows. But he's in the best of hands, and we'll do everything we humanly can to save him. Meanwhile, I want you to ring a reliable friend and ask them to bring in Jessie's favourite things, a bear maybe, his blanket from his bed? Reassuring stuff. The paramedics will have informed the police. Tell your friend not to go near the house until he's sure the police have the dog under control.'

'The dog's a pussy cat,' the man said, brokenly.

'No,' Luke said grimly. 'He's a dog. And your son…' He closed his eyes for a fraction of a moment and when he opened them Lily saw something behind his eyes that looked like pain. 'Jessie,' he said. 'It's up to us now to see if we can save your Jessie.'

She'd come on duty tonight as an unknown nurse, expecting to be treated as very junior. In fact, she'd kind of wanted to be junior. Anonymous. Working steadily in the background, a tiny cog in a big wheel, disappearing as soon as she was off duty, coming on duty tomorrow on another ward, knowing no one, no one knowing her. Bliss.

What she hadn't expected was to be part of a close-knit, highly skilled team, working desperately to save one little life.

That weird conversation she'd overheard in Admin was put aside. For some reason Luke had been checking her credentials. Whether the conversation between Finn and Luke should have the pair of them up before the medical board for sexual discrimination was immaterial right now. What was important was that Luke knew she was up to the job in hand and he let the rest of the team know it. The hospital was desperately short-staffed, so she was no doormat, standing in the background. She was scrub nurse, working with every ounce of her knowledge and skill.

They all were.

The child's face had been torn from chin to forehead. A vast flap of skin and flesh was hanging from his cheek. Among the blood and mess, they could see bone.

His eye socket, his nose, the side of his mouth… Unspeakable damage…

But the flesh hadn't been ripped away entirely. If Luke had the skills he might…he must…

The alternative was unthinkable. If the flap couldn't be replaced, this little boy would be facing years of grafts, even a face transplant. A life of immuno-suppressant drugs. If he lived.

The alternative was that Luke sorted this mangled mess and teased it all back into place. That he keep the flap alive, re-establish blood supply, leave nerves undamaged…

A miracle?

No. Pure skill.

Her initial impressions of the man were that he was…okay, a womaniser. He'd been laughing with her. Eyeing her appreciatively. Talking with the director of surgery about her in *that* way…

Now every speck of concentration was on what he was doing. Jessie's face was an intricate jigsaw puzzle that had to be fitted together before the blood supply was compromised. Every tiny torn piece had to be sorted, cleaned, put into careful, cautious position.

The nursing team of the hospital might have been hit by gastro but there was no hint of understaffing now. This was priority one, a child's life. Luke was assisted by a surgical registrar, a paediatric anaesthetist, two scrub nurses and two junior nurses. All were totally focused.

And in their hands was a little boy called Jessie. Red-headed. Freckled on the tiny part of his face that wasn't damaged. He was intubated, heavily anaesthetised. He'd been lucky he hadn't drowned in his own blood.

Every person in the room was totally tuned to what they were doing. This was the most important job in the world, saving a child's life…piece by piece…

Lily thought briefly of a case she'd worked on three years back. A professor in Adelaide, trying to save a man's lips. Problems with drainage afterwards. Like Luke, the professor's total attention had been caught in what he was doing, but afterwards he'd talked through what might have helped.

She turned to the closest junior nurse.

'Slip out and find Dr Lockheart,' she said. 'Tell her we may need medical leeches. Tell her priority one.'

'I don't have authority…' the girl said, casting a worried glance at Luke, but Luke's attention was all on what he was doing. He might not have the head space to think beyond his current actions, Lily thought.

The anaesthetist, the registrar, the senior scrub nurse were totally focused as well.

'Just say leeches are needed urgently,' she told the nurse. There was no need to say the agency temp had ordered them. 'Be it on my head if they're not.'

And it would be her head, too, she thought. Leeches were kept in only a few medical facilities around the country. Her order might well involve helicopter, urgency, cost.

So sack me, she thought grimly, and went back to what she was doing. Elaine, the senior scrub nurse, needed to back off a little; there was only so long that she could hold the suction tube steady, that her fingers would do as she bid.

Luke's fingers didn't have a choice, they had to keep going.

'Lily, move in,' Luke growled, and he'd sensed it too, that the older nurse was faltering.

She moved in and kept on going.

Two hours later her decision was vindicated. The flap of skin was finally closed around the nostril and left lip. Luke was working under the little boy's eyelid but he rechecked the lip and swore.

'The blood's coagulating,' he said. 'I need drainage. Hell, I didn't think we'd get this far.'

'We have leeches on hand if you can use them,' she said diffidently, and the nurse in the background was already unfastening the canister.

'How the…?' Luke was momentarily distracted. 'Did Dr Lockheart order these?'

'Lily did,' the junior said, and grinned, the atmosphere in the theatre lightening as the outlook improved. 'She's not bad for an agency temp, is she?'

'Not bad at all,' Luke said, and caught Lily's gaze and held, just for a moment, a fleeting second, before he went back to work.

Lily went back to work, too, but she was flushing under her mask.

*Not bad at all.*

His glance had unnerved her.

Luke Williams was a womanising surgeon, she told herself. She was here as a temporary nurse, knowing no one, wanting to know no one.

But his gaze…

It did something to her insides. Twisted…

She didn't have time for anything to twist.

Work. Anonymity. Just do what comes next.

At five in the morning she was totally drained.

'Go home,' Dr Lockheart told her. 'We've thrown you in at the deep end tonight. I know you're not off duty until six but no one's expecting anything more of you now.

'And if you'd like to change agency nursing for permanent nursing at the Harbour, you'd be very,

very welcome,' Elaine said warmly. 'Dr Williams is already asking that you be made a permanent member of the plastics team.'

'I don't want to be a permanent member of anything,' she said wearily, and went to change and fetch her gear from her locker.

Home.

Problem. She didn't actually have a home. Not until ten o'clock.

She'd arrived in Sydney yesterday, fresh from her mother's dramas, wanting only to escape.

Her mother was, even by Lily's dutiful daughter standards, an impossible woman. She drifted from drama to drama, and the small town they lived in had labelled her as trash, for good reason. She wasn't trash, Lily thought. She was…needy. She needed men. And in between needing men, she needed Lily.

This last fling, though, had pushed the townspeople to the limit. It had pushed Lily to the limit. Two days ago—had it really been only two days ago?— the wife of the local vicar, a woman who was also the head of the hospital board, had stormed into Lighthouse Cove hospital and slapped her. As if her mother's actions were Lily's fault.

'Get your mother away from my husband. You and your mother… She's a slut and you're no better. She needs a leash! You think you can be a respectable nurse in this town while your mother acts as the town's whore?' She'd slapped Lily again. A couple of patients' relatives had had to pull her away and she'd collapsed in shock and in fury. Lily had caught her as she'd fallen, stopped her from hurting herself, but there had been no gratitude. No softening of the vitriol.

Why would there be?

'Get out of my sight,' the woman had hissed as she'd recovered. 'Get out of our hospital. Get out of our town.'

She'd had no right to sack her. It was her mother who'd played the scarlet woman, not her.

But in a tiny town distinctions blurred.

She'd sat in the nurses' station with her stomach cramping, feeling sick, knowing she couldn't live with this stress a moment longer. She was being unfairly tarred with the same brush as her mother, and she knew she didn't deserve it. But it was a small town and so far she'd always stuck up for her mother...that couldn't go on.

On the way home she'd stopped to buy groceries. Walking into the general store had been a nightmare. Shocked, judgmental faces had been everywhere.

*The Ellis women.*

Then she'd tried to use her card to pay for groceries. 'Declined: Limit exceeded.'

*Her mother had been using her credit card?*

Speechless, she'd gone home and there was the vicar, pudgy, weak and shamefaced, but totally besotted with her mother.

'Make yourself scarce for a while, there's a good girl,' her mother had said. 'We need time to ourselves. It'll be okay, dear,' she'd cooed as Lily had tried to figure what to do, what to say. 'We were going to go to Paris but we've run out of money. It doesn't matter. If Harold can just borrow a little bit more from his relatives we'll leave. We're in love and everyone just needs time to accept it.'

Enough. What had followed had been the world's fastest pack. She'd driven eight hundred and fifty miles from Adelaide to Sydney. A seventeen-hour drive, her stomach cramping all the way. She'd had cat naps at the side of the road, or she'd tried to, but sleep had refused to come. She'd arrived in Sydney late in the afternoon, trying to figure how she could survive on what little money she had.

She'd walked into the nursing agency before it had closed and they'd fallen on her neck.

'All your documents and references are in order. There's a job tonight, if you're available. Sydney Harbour Hospital is desperate.'

She'd found a cheap boarding house, dumped her luggage and booked accommodation for the next night. That was tonight, she thought, glancing at her watch. She could have the room from ten.

But it was five hours until ten o'clock, and she was so tired she was asleep on her feet.

Her stomach hurt.

She stared at her locker, trying to make her mind think. The thought of finding an all-hours café until then made her feel ill. There'd be an on-call room somewhere for medical staff, she thought. Probably there'd be a few. There'd be rooms for obstetricians waiting for babies. Rooms for surgeons waiting for their turn in complex multi-specialist procedures.

Rooms to sleep?

Just for a couple of hours, she thought. Just until it was a reasonable time to find breakfast and book into her boarding house.

Just for now.

He had a whole hour of thinking he'd done it right. One lousy hour and then the phone went off beside his bed.

'Problem.' It was Finn. Of course it was Finn— when did the man ever sleep?

When did Finn ever wake him when it wasn't a full-blown emergency? Luke was hauling his pants on before Finn's next words.

'It's Jessie,' Finn snapped. 'It seems he has a congenital heart problem. No one thought to tell us, not that it would have made a difference to what you did anyway. His heart's failing. You want to come in or you want me to deal?'

'I'm on my way.'

She woke and he was right beside her. Luke Williams, plastic surgeon. He looked like he'd just seen death.

The on-call room was tiny, one big squishy settee, a television, a coffee table with ancient magazines and nothing else. She'd curled into a corner of the couch and fallen asleep. Until now.

The man beside her wasn't seeing her. He was staring at the blank television screen, gaze unfocused.

She'd never seen a man look so bleak.

'What's wrong?' she breathed, and touched his arm.

He flinched.

'What are you doing here?' His voice was harsh. Breaking. It was emotion that had woken her, she thought. Raw grief, filling the room like a tangible thing.

'I don't get into my boarding house until ten,' she told him. 'So I'm camped out, waiting. But what is it? Jessie?'

'He died,' he said, and all the bleakness in the world was in those two words. 'Cardiac arrest. He had a congenital heart problem and no one thought to tell us. As if we had time to look for records. The admission officer didn't even read the form, she was too upset. We patched him up, we made him look like he might even be okay, and all the time his heart was like a time bomb.'

'There was no choice,' she managed, appalled.

'There was a choice. If I'd known…I could have taken the flap off, thought about grafts later, concentrated on getting his heart stable first.'

She took a deep breath. What to say?

This man's anguish was raw and real.

A congenital heart problem…

If Luke had known he might well have decided not to try and save his face, but without that immediate operation Jess would have been left with a lifetime of skin grafts. With a face that wasn't his.

'What sort of life would he have led?' she whispered.

'A life,' he said flatly. 'Any life. I can't bear…'

And she couldn't bear it either. She took his hands and tugged him around to face her.

There was more to this than a child dying, she thought. This man must have lost patients before. He couldn't react like this to all of them. There was some past tragedy here that was being tapped into, she guessed. She had no idea what it was; but she sensed his pain was well nigh unbearable.

'I killed him,' he said, and for some reason she wasn't sure he was talking about Jessie.

'The dog killed him,' she said, trying to sound prosaic. 'You tried to save him.'

'I should have—'

'No. Don't do this.'

He shuddered, and it was a raw and dreadful grief that took over his whole body.

Enough. She pulled him into her arms and held him. And held and held. She simply held him while the shudders racked his body, over and over.

This couldn't just be about this child, she thought. Something had broken him.

He was holding her as well now. Simply holding. Taking strength from her. Taking comfort, and giving it back.

A man and a woman, both in limbo.

The events of the past two days had left Lily gutted. Her mother… The vicar…. Losing her job. The judgement of the town.

*The Ellis women.*

She held to comfort, but he was holding her as well and she needed it.

Jessie's death. The trauma of finding what her mother had done, planned to do. Forty-eight hours with little sleep.

If she could give comfort…

If this was what they both needed…

He shouldn't be here. He shouldn't be holding this woman.

But he wasn't thinking of now. He was thinking of Jessie, four years old and red-headed.

The past was back with him. Four years ago, walking into their apartment after surgery that had lasted for fourteen hours. Exhausted but jubilant. Calling out to Hannah. 'I'm home. It's over and she'll live. Hannah…'

Walking into the bedroom

Ectopic pregnancy, the autopsy said. Fourteen weeks pregnant.

By her side, a letter to her mother in Canada.

*'Tonight I'm finally telling Luke I'm pregnant. I've been waiting and waiting—I thought a lovely romantic dinner, but there's no chance. He's been so busy it's driving me crazy but now he'll have to make time for us. I want a son. I'm hoping he'll be red-headed like me. I want to call him Jessie.'*

Tonight, four years later, he hadn't been able to save a red-headed boy called Jessie.

The woman in his arms was holding him. She smelled clean, washed, anonymous, clinical.

But more. The scent of faded roses was drifting through, like some afterthought of a lovely perfume. The silken threads of her fair hair were brushing his face.

She was an agency nurse. She didn't know him.

She was warm and real and alive.

He'd come in here to sit, to try and come to terms with what had happened. He had two hours before his morning list started. He needed to get himself under control

Jessie.

Hannah.

They were nothing to do with the woman who was holding him.

She shuddered and he thought, She's as shocked as I am. He tugged away a little and searched her face.

Her sky-blue eyes were rimmed with shadows. Her shock mirrored his. She looked like she, too, was in the midst of a nightmare.

'Lily…' It was the first time he'd used her name and it felt like…a question?

'Don't,' she said. 'Just hold me. Please.' And she tugged him back to her.

He should back away.

He didn't. He couldn't. He simply held. And held and held.

A man and a woman—with a need surfacing between them as primeval as time itself.

Stupid. Crazy. Wanton?

It didn't matter. It couldn't matter.

His hands were slipping under her blouse, feeling the warmth of her, the heat. He needed her heat.

Her breasts were moulding to his chest. Skin was meeting skin, and conscious will was slipping. Their bodies were meeting, in a desperate, primitive search for...

What?

For life?

That was a crazy idea. He was crazy.

It didn't matter.

For now, for this moment, he was kissing her, holding her, wanting her, with a desperation that was so deep, so real that nothing could interfere.

They were only kissing. They were only holding. They were only touching.

No. This was much, much more. This was a man and a woman come together in mutual need, giving, taking...

Holding desperately to life.

'Luke...'

'Just hold me,' he ordered, and she did, she did. She held.

Fire to fire. Need to need.

They held—and two minutes later a junior nurse looking for something to read in her coffee break slipped into the room and saw two entwined bodies.

One passionate embrace.

The girl stared, dumbfounded, as she realised who it was. The solitary Luke Williams. Head of Plastic Surgery. A man who walked alone.

*Kissing an agency nurse. Slipping his hands under her blouse.*

*And, oh, that kiss...*

She gasped in disbelief and backed out, her magazine forgotten.

Who needed magazines when there was much better fodder right through the door? Boy, was this juicy titbit about to fly around the hospital.

# CHAPTER THREE

LILY had signed up for four weeks at Sydney Harbour. That was approximately three weeks and six days too long. She knew it the moment she turned up for duty that night. Gossip reached her the moment she crossed the threshold.

From the lady in the florist shop on the ground floor, to the orderlies, to the nurses and interns working in Emergency where she'd been rostered, it seemed they all knew what had happened that morning.

They didn't know her—many of them hadn't even been working last night—but they knew Luke Williams and it seemed the gossip machine was in overdrive.

A mutual offering of comfort had turned to something stronger, and the hospital gossip machine had flamed the story to the next level. Even before she'd walked out this morning she'd realised the news was flying all over the hospital—that she and

Luke Williams had indulged in wild sex in the on-call room.

It had taken sheer willpower to walk back into the Harbour tonight—plus the fact that, thanks to her mother, she was broke. She'd agreed to four weeks and if she didn't fulfil her contract she'd have to find another agency. This was the only agency that dealt with acute-care hospitals and she didn't have the money to leave Sydney.

The alternative was to go back home to her mother. And the vicar.

No way.

So get over it, she told herself. She'd been caught in a clinch with the head of plastic surgery. So what? Who cared what these people talked about? In four weeks she could pick up her pay and move on.

How far did she have to run to escape gossip?

For ever if she brought it with her, she told herself, keeping her chin deliberately high. What had she been thinking, letting Luke hold her as he had? She was just like her mother.

Um…no. Her mother would never do what she'd done. Her mother would now be declaring to the world that she was in love, and she'd be destroying anything and anyone she needed in order to get what she wanted. Her mother would get her heart broken and launch herself into suicidal depression when it was over.

Lily had simply made one mistake. She'd been emotionally shattered and she'd fallen into the arms of someone who was equally shattered.

There was no need for everyone to look at her sideways.

They did anyway.

'Wow.' Elaine, a woman who'd looked intimidating and severe last night, relaxed enough to greet her with laughter as she appeared at the nurses' station. 'Who's on your list tonight?' Then at Lily's expression her smile softened; becoming friendly. 'Don't look like that. Lots of women in this place would offer to comfort Luke Williams any way they know how. That man is a walking suit of armour. I don't know how you managed it but his armour was well and truly pierced last night, and thank heaven for it. Maybe now he can move on.'

'Move on?'

'You didn't know?' Obviously things were quiet right now, because the senior nurse was ready to talk. 'Luke's wife died four years ago. She was gorgeous, a redhead with a temper to match. She had an ectopic pregnancy, went into septic shock and died, and Luke didn't even know she was pregnant. Since then it's been like he's built the Great Wall of China around himself. No one gets near. And then you did.'

'I don't usually…' she managed.

'Nobody gives a toss what you usually do,' Elaine said. 'The fact is that our mighty Dr Williams has been shagged by an agency nurse.'

*'I did not…'*

'It doesn't matter whether you did or didn't,' Elaine said bluntly. 'Gossip is truth as far as this hospital is concerned, and we're delighted. Let him try and keep his armour after this. A girl with accommodating morals was just what he needed. Now… we've just got word there's been a boat crash on the harbour, two guys with suspected spinal injuries and a girl with deep facial lacerations expected any minute. I suspect we'll want you in Theatre again. Scrub?'

'I… Yes.' At least this was a vote of confidence. She'd expected to be treated like a pariah. Here she was being handed a position of responsibility.

'You did great last night,' Elaine said. 'In more ways than one. But hands off the rest of our male staff, at least until you're off duty. You've done us a favour with our Luke, but let's not push things too far.'

And that was that.

*A girl with accommodating morals...* Everyone was looking at her.

Aaagh.

He'd come close to having sex with an unknown nurse in the on-call room. It was like being a member of the mile-high club, he thought. Sordid and stupid.

Only it hadn't felt like that at the time.

But that's how his colleagues were treating it, as a huge joke. Medics had black humour at the best of times. Jessie's death last night had upset them all and Luke's out-of-character behaviour was a welcome diversion.

Even Finn commented. 'About time,' he growled. 'Now take her out properly and do it again.'

Huh? He didn't date. Ever.

He wasn't starting now.

What had happened? He'd been gutted by the events of the night; he'd found himself in the on-call room simply because he hadn't had the strength to get back to his apartment without getting some sort of grip on himself, and she'd been there.

He'd lost himself in holding her. She'd felt…

Amazing. Just amazing. From a night where all he could see was black, he'd been lifted into a world of warmth, and strength and laughter. Yes, even laughter. She'd made a gentle joke as the world intruded, she hadn't let him apologise, she'd slipped away and he'd thought he might not even see her again.

What would have happened if they hadn't been interrupted? He should feel grateful that they had been—they'd both been well out of control. Instead, strangely, he felt an empty regret. And worry for her. The gossip machine in this hospital was ruthless.

When he'd finished his day's list he'd gone back to the agency sheet, checked for her address and found a simple 'To be advised'. So he couldn't find her even if he wanted to. She was an agency nurse. She might not even turn up tonight.

She did.

Evie called him at dusk.

'Your lady's back. She's contracted to us for four weeks. Are you popping into Emergency tonight by any chance?'

Evie was laughing.

'I might,' he conceded.

'To introduce yourself?' Evie was definitely laughing.

'What makes you think I don't know her?' he growled before he could stop himself.

'You know her? I thought this was lust at first sight.'

'Leave it alone,' he told her. 'I'm coming in.'

'The lady's busy,' Evie said. 'We're run off our feet. She goes off duty at six; you can come and take her home.'

They met before that. The woman with lacerations needed someone with real skill if she wasn't to be scarred for life. Once again he found himself in Theatre, with Lily as second scrub.

This wasn't a life-and-death situation. Becky Martin would survive with barely a scar from her drunken joy ride in a powerboat, and the mood in the theatre was a far cry from last night's trauma.

But it was also a far cry from the usual relaxed theatre. Everyone was watching Luke—and Lily. One glance between them and it'd start again.

No. They didn't even have to glance for the gossip to keep going, Luke thought. This hospital used gossip as a means to dispel tension, and what they'd done last night had started a wildfire that only time would extinguish.

Or Lily leaving.

She might. She looked strained and flushed.

She was working with professional competence, anticipating well, displaying skills he valued. Even so, he wasn't sure he wanted her here. He didn't like his staff distracted and they were distracted by her.

That wasn't fair, he thought grimly. She was being judged because she'd tried to comfort him.

His colleagues thought his actions were amusing. They saw her as…easy.

That was a harsh judgement by any standards.

He put in the last suture, stood back from the table and sighed.

'Well done, Luke,' his anaesthetist said. 'Great job. You deserve a wee rest. I hear the on-call room's free. Nurse Ellis, maybe you're free, too?'

'Leave it,' he growled, and watched in concern as Lily started to clear.

The junior nurse was sniggering.

He needed to talk to her, he thought. He needed to apologise.

Not in the on-call room.

He was due to sleep. Lily was on duty all night. He'd come in at change-over, he decided. He'd see her then.

*Not in the on-call room.*

Luke disappeared and she could get on with her night's work. Which was just as well. The guy was distracting, to say the least, and the staff reaction was well nigh unbearable. With him gone she could lose herself in what needed to be done.

She felt mortified. She was also feeling…ill? Her stomach cramps were getting worse, and now there was nausea on top of them.

She'd left Lighthouse Cove to get rid of the tension that was making her sick. In two days here, she'd only created more tension.

'You're looking pale,' Elaine said in passing. 'You'd better not be coming down with gastro. Half this hospital's had it, but I thought we were past the worst. Are you feeling okay?'

'I'm just tired,' Lily said. 'I've had a hard…' She caught Elaine's gaze and stopped. 'I mean…'

'No, no, I understand,' Elaine said, grinning. 'You and Luke… I'd imagine he can be very tiring. But according to Dr Blain, who heard it from Dr Lockheart, word is you already know him. Is that right? Why did you make me tell you about him if you're old friends?'

'I—'

'I know he keeps to himself, but if he pairs up with someone who does the same thing we're in real trouble,' Elaine said. 'Apparently he's coming to take you home at six. If you make it that long.' Her eyes narrowed. 'You're looking sick as a dog. Tell you what, you stick round the nurses' station until handover and finish the paperwork there. If you're coming down with gastro, we don't want you near patients.'

'I'm just tired—and I don't need anyone to take me home.'

'It's not anyone, it's Luke Williams. Paperwork for you, my girl, and then let your lover take you home to bed.'

Lily had felt bad before. She tackled her paperwork feeling infinitely worse.

Luke found her in the locker room, preparing to leave.

He could have gone the whole four weeks of her contract without seeing her again, he thought. With the gastro outbreak almost over, staff levels were nearly back to normal. He could easily arrange for her not to be rostered to Theatre with him.

He could pretend the encounter had never happened.

Finn used women to forget, Luke thought. Maybe he could, too.

Only…there was something about Lily that made him think it hadn't been a casual embrace. That her need had been almost as great as his.

A lesser man wouldn't need to ask why, but for some reason this didn't feel like a simple matter of honour. It was how she'd made him feel. It had been the generosity of her body, the smile behind her eyes, the touch of her…

He'd remember it, he thought, and he honoured her for it.

And she was being labelled because of it. The least he could do was thank her and apologise.

He opened the locker-room door and she turned to face him. She looked white faced. A bit unsteady on her feet. Wobbling?

He crossed the room in four long strides to reach her. Gripped her shoulders. Steadied her.

'Hey…'

'It's…it's okay,' she said, and hauled away to plonk herself down on the wooden bench. 'I'm just having a queasy moment.'

'You're not pregnant, are you?'

She gave him a look that would have withered lesser men. It was the look he deserved.

What had made him say that? Of all the ridiculous…

'We didn't make it that far, Superman,' she retorted. 'You don't get pregnant by kissing, no matter how hot you think you are.'

'I'm sorry,' he said, with feeling. 'That was dumb. Plus offensive. But you're ill.'

'I suspect,' she said with as much dignity as she could muster, 'that I'm coming down with this blasted gastroenteritis that half this hospital seems to have suffered. You should have a huge skull and crossbones on the entrance with a sign saying "Abandon hope all ye who enter here".'

'Or abandon the contents of your stomach.'

'Don't,' she begged. 'Go away.'

'Let me take you home.'

She glared. 'Tell me you don't have a car with leather upholstery and I might be interested.'

'I do,' he admitted. 'But we can go via Emergency and get a supply of sick bags. I had it last week so I won't get infected.'

'You might have infected me.'

'Then that'd be yet another thing I need to apologise for,' he said grimly, and took her elbows, propelling her up. 'We'll organise you a shot of metoclopramide for the nausea. Then we'll take some paper bags and take you home and to bed.'

'No.'

'No?'

'I mean, yes, please,' she said with as much dignity as she could muster. 'Only I need to spend ten minutes in the bathroom first.'

They didn't speak on the way to the address she'd given him. She didn't lose her dignity, but he could see she was holding onto it with every shred of effort she could muster. One shot of metoclopramide was barely holding it.

She wasn't what she'd seemed. Questions were crowding in, but his medical training told him that breaking her concentration would be unwise. So he focused on driving, found the address, pulled up in front of a boarding house that looked as if it had seen better days and watched in astonishment as she struggled out of the car.

'You don't live here?'

'No,' she said, closing the car door with care, as if it was a really tricky task. 'I'm staying here. Thank you for bringing me home.' And she headed for the gate.

He was out of the car, through the gate, stopping her.

'Don't stop me,' she pleaded. 'I need…'

'I know this place,' he said. 'When I was an intern we averaged one drug overdose a week from this dump.'

She was trying to shove past him, looking increasingly desperate. 'It's only until payday. It has a bathroom. Please…'

She was nothing to do with him, he told himself. This was none of his business. He'd brought her home. He'd done what he had to do.

But…she'd held him. She'd stopped his grief from stripping him raw.

She'd lightened his life.

That had to be an overstatement, he told himself. One crazy impulse did not mean emotional change. She'd simply been there when he'd needed her, had responded to his need, had maybe used him to assuage her own needs.

Her own needs were pretty apparent now. She'd broken from him and was doubled over behind a scrubby hedge. The garden was filthy.

Questions.

She was a skilled theatre nurse from a town he remembered as being quiet and beautiful.

His colleagues had her labelled as wanton.

She'd held him.

Whatever she was, he couldn't leave her here.

She was crouched, trembling, in the filthy garden, sweaty and sick, and he knew he had no choice.

He waited for the spasms to cease. Then, giving her no chance to argue, he stooped and lifted her into his arms and carried her back to his car. He deposited her back into the passenger seat before she knew what he was doing.

'What's your room number?' he demanded.

'T-twelve.' She could barely speak. 'But—'

'Give me your key.'

'I don't…'

He took her purse from her limp grasp and retrieved the key.

'Don't argue and don't move,' he said, and headed for the house.

She didn't go anywhere. How could she? That last episode had left her wanting to do nothing so much as to lie down and die. Her bed in the boarding house was lumpy and none too clean, but it was a bed and right now she wanted it more than anything else in the world. Only her legs didn't feel like they'd take her anywhere.

After the week she'd had, it needed only this. Of all the stupid hospitals she had to temp in, it had to be Sydney Harbour Hospital during a gastro epidemic.

She wanted to die.

Why was she sitting in Luke's car?

It was too hard to do anything else.

She closed her eyes and he was back again, carrying her suitcase. That got through…sort of. 'What…?' She was trying to get her thoughts in order. She wasn't succeeding.

'You're not staying here,' Luke said grimly. 'This place is drug bust central.' Then his face sort of…

changed. He slid into the driver's seat and pushed up her uniform sleeves.

She got that. No matter that she was dying...*he thought she was a crackhead*?

Enough. There were some things up with which a girl did not put. Or something. She wasn't making sense even to herself, but as he tried to check her pupils she found the strength to haul back her hand and slap him. Straight across his cheek with all the strength she could muster. Which wasn't actually very much. He recoiled but not far, then caught her hands in his before she could do it again.

'Just checking,' he said, mildly.

'I drink champagne every time I get a pay rise,' she managed through gritted teeth. 'I'm addicted to romance novels and chocolate. I once got a speeding ticket and a parking fine all in the one month. Evil doesn't begin to describe me—*but I don't do drugs.*' She tried, very badly, not to sob, as she hauled her hands away from his and fumbled for the door catch.

'No.' He leaned over and tugged the door closed, took her shoulders and twisted her to face him. 'I'm sorry.'

'Me, too. Let me out.'

'I'm taking you home.'

'I am home.'

'My home.'

'You don't want a junkie at home.'

'You're not a junkie,' he said wearily. 'I've seen enough to know I've mortally offended you. Can I start making amends?'

'There's no need…' But her stomach wasn't up to arguing. Another cramp hit and she doubled over.

He handed her a paper bag but she didn't need it. There was nothing left.

He waited for the spasms to cease, then magically produced moist wipes. 'Paper bags and wipes from Emergency,' he said softly as he cupped her chin in one hand and washed her face. She was so limp she couldn't argue. 'You get parking tickets. I steal wipes. Criminals both. You want to do a Thelma and Louise and run for the border?'

'I… No.'

'Thought not,' he said, and fastened her seat belt for her. 'Let's find you an alternative.'

His surgical list started at eight and he made it only fifteen minutes late. This morning was his private list, cosmetic surgery. The woman he was treating had travelled overseas to get cheek implants, a re-shaped nose and liposuction for her thighs. She'd got what she'd paid for and she hadn't paid much. She'd ended up with a perforation of the nasal septum, a nasal obstruction and nasal deformity. One of her cheek implants had slipped, which meant her face was weirdly lopsided and her thighs were...undulating. She had lumps and bumps all over the place.

He wasn't working on her legs this morning. He'd remove the cheek implants first—he wasn't the least sure of their quality and the last thing she needed was one to burst. Then he needed to focus on revision rhinoplasty and repair of the septal perforation.

She'd need further procedures and he couldn't be sure she'd look as good as she had when she'd started.

Cosmetic surgery could sometimes be brilliant, restoring self-image, but this time it had been a disaster.

The surgery he'd had as a child had been brilliant.

Luke's childhood had been made miserable by a massive port wine birthmark almost covering one side of his face. His parents, cold and emotionally detached, had decreed it was simply 'character building', but when he'd been fourteen his uncle had stepped in.

'I've arranged the best plastic surgeon I can afford,' he'd told his father. 'The kid's getting that off his face whether you like it or not.'

His uncle was a bachelor, taciturn, unsentimental, refusing thanks. He and the plastic surgeon he'd found had changed Luke's life and had set him on the path he was on now.

His uncle's farm had been lifesaving as well. It still was. Even though his uncle was as emotionally distant as the rest of his family, his farm had been a retreat from the world.

He hadn't been to the farm for two weeks now and he was missing it. Maybe he could take off for a few days. Leave his apartment to Lily. Whoever Lily was.

Not a junkie. An unanswered question.

Don't get close.

'So tell me about your lady of the night.' Finn's voice from the doorway to his office made him start. Dammit, he should be used to it. He wasn't. 'My what?'

'Your one-night stand. Or your one-morning stand. You planning to make it two mornings?'

'Leave it,' he growled. He thought of Lily as he'd left her, huddled in his bed, so sick she could hardly acknowledge he was leaving. He'd stayed with her for an hour and made sure the retching had stopped. He'd left her with fluids, and he knew all she needed was sleep, but still he'd hated leaving her.

And somehow…for some reason he hated this hospital thinking she was…his one-night stand.

Sydney Harbour Hospital. It should read Sydney

Scandal Central, he thought. Any hint of gossip was through the place in minutes. A team of skilled medics working long hours under intense pressure, in teams where they were thrown together in emotionally charged scenarios over and over, made for a hotbed of scandal. Up until now he hadn't added to it.

It drove him crazy, though, the fact that he was being watched all the time. 'When's our aloof Dr Williams going to crack and prove he's human?'

He was aware he was a target; he was aware there were bets—first woman to break his icy barricade. Even a couple of the gay guys had tried.

The gossips would be relentless now, he thought. A one-night stand… They wouldn't stop.

And Lily? She'd signed up for four weeks' work and she was labelled from this moment forth.

She was in his bed. They'd find that out in about two seconds flat. Other medics lived in his apartment block, Kirribilli Views. Hell, his cleaning lady was due in there this afternoon. By the time she'd finished dusting, the news would be all over Sydney.

'She's not a one-night stand,' he found himself saying, before he even knew he intended saying it. 'I already told Dr Lockheart that. I've known Lily for years.'

'Years?' Finn raised his brows in disbelief. Finn Kennedy made stronger doctors than Luke nervous,

Luke thought. The man just had to raise one of those supercilious eyebrows and minions were supposed to quake.

But Luke was still thinking of Lily retching. This was no time for quaking. Or for disbelief.

'Why do you think she's here?' he demanded. 'We wanted to see if we could make a go of it.'

'You were checking her records.'

'I was making sure they'd got her address right. We used a boarding-house address as cover, intending to keep our relationship private a bit longer.'

'By snogging on the on-call couch?'

'Yeah, that wasn't exactly wise,' he admitted. 'She was waiting for me after finishing work. I found her and…' He closed his eyes. 'The kid had just died. Sure, what happened was inappropriate, but Lily's a big-hearted woman. She held me first, asked questions later.'

'You're in a relationship. What the—?'

'This hospital thinks it knows everything about me,' Luke said wearily. 'It doesn't.'

The door to his office was open. Their voices were carrying, which was just what Luke intended.

Everyone knew what had happened in the on-call room. They were labelling Lily because of it, but if they thought Lily and Luke were in an established relationship she'd be treated with respect. He'd already hinted at it to Evie. Why not take it further?

Maybe this was the least he could do. Where women were concerned he always did the least he could do, he thought grimly, but this time…

'You bring your woman to work here without telling us about the relationship?' For some reason Finn's disbelief was giving way to anger.

'What of it?' It was Evie, just passing. Like half the hospital. How many medics used this corridor, and how carrying was Finn's voice?

Answer—very carrying.

'It's deception,' Finn growled.

'What, not telling us who he's sleeping with?' Evie demanded. 'What gives us the right to know?'

'We're a team.'

'If we are you have an odd way of treating team members,' Evie snapped. 'Leave Luke alone. It's his business.'

'If he wants to bring his—'

'Luke's your friend,' Evie said, closing the door. 'You want to make this worse?'

'I have a patient being sedated,' Luke said warily. Sparks flew whenever these two got close and he didn't want to be in the middle. He needed to leave. Now.

'I'm so pleased,' Evie was saying warmly, and she

hugged him. 'She's a very competent nurse. I agree you should have told us, but...' she cast a disparaging glance at Finn '...I can see why you wouldn't. She looked bad though when she left this morning. Is she okay?'

'She has gastro,' Luke said. 'Remind me to speak to Admin. She'll have got it here; she'll get paid for time off or I'll take it further.'

'She needs time off?'

'Yes.'

'Where is she now?' Finn growled, and Luke fixed his friend with a challenging stare.

'At home,' he said. 'In my bed.'

'How wonderful,' Evie said happily. 'Lily and Luke... Ooh, I love it.' She cast a cheeky look at Finn. 'Maybe it's time you tried a solid relationship, Mr Kennedy.'

'In your dreams,' Finn snapped.

'Aren't you having one?' Luke asked.

'He's been seen with Mariette from Accounts,' Evie said, disparagingly. 'Not exactly a long-term proposition, that one.'

'Will you butt out?' Finn was almost explosive.

'Like you butted out of Luke's love life?' Evie retorted. 'Certainly, Mr Kennedy. Can I walk you to Theatre, Dr Williams?'

'Yes,' Luke said with relief.

'And tell me about Lily on the way. Leave nothing out. First sight, first touch, first kiss. The whole romantic fantasy.'

Fantasy, Luke thought. She had it right there.

Lily woke as someone was vacuuming right through the door.

There were sunbeams on her counterpane. *Her counterpane?*

She was lying in the middle of a king-sized bed, on down-filled pillows, ensconced in crisp, white sheets and fleecy blankets.

The room was spacious, painted in cool soft greys, with white drapes—masculine but not too harsh.

The focus of the room was the floor-length picture windows, and through the windows Sydney Harbour.

She could see the Manly ferry chugging across the harbour. She could see the opera house.

A sunbeam was on her nose.

The cramps had stopped. She wriggled, very carefully. The nausea had gone as well.

She'd died and gone to heaven.

She was in Luke Williams's bed.

It didn't matter whose bed she was in, she decided. Anyone with a bed like this was a friend for life.

Was she more like her mother than she'd thought?

Even that concept wasn't enough to spoil what she was feeling right now. Like life might be possible again.

A tap on the door. 'Come in.' She hauled her sheets to her chin, expecting...Luke? Instead a chubby little lady in a floral pinafore peered round the door, looking anxious.

'Are you awake, dear? I didn't want to disturb you, only I popped my nose round the door an hour ago and saw you hadn't drunk anything. I think Dr Williams would like you to drink. Would you like a cup of tea?'

Lily thought about it. She had many things to think about, but right now tea was pretty much the limit of her brain power.

'I'd love one.'

'With lots of sugar.' The lady beamed. 'I'm Gladys Henderson and I do for Dr Williams. I do for other doctors in this apartment block as well but he's my favourite. But he's in my bad books for not telling me you were coming. They tell me you've had quite the romance and then you just start doing night duty and no one knew. And now to get this nasty bug... But we're all so pleased for Dr Williams. He's ever so nice and we've been thinking he goes up to that farm of his all the time with only his old uncle, and he stares at nothing and just thinks and thinks about that poor young wife of his. But she's four years dead, and we're so pleased…well, not pleased she's dead, of course, but pleased as Punch that he's got a young lady. And that's enough from me; you don't want me standing here gabbling for ever. I'll make you a nice cup of tea and plump your pillows and then you settle down and sleep until the doctor comes home. Ooh, I do love a good romance.'

# CHAPTER FOUR

LUKE'S list went overtime. There were always complications, he thought. The problem with being a plastic surgeon with a decent reputation was that he was sent other people's mistakes. Repairs of repairs… He hated it.

His real work, his passion, was repairs that made a huge difference to people's lives. Birth defects, accidents, improving the aesthetic results after disfiguring cancer surgery.

He'd refused at first to do cosmetic surgery but there was a need. The lines blurred between vanity and distress and he couldn't say no.

Regardless, he left the hospital as he always did on a Wednesdays, feeling that his time could be better utilised. Feeling that there should be something more.

Like going home to Hannah and their little boy?

No. Time had left him ceasing to miss Hannah. In truth, their marriage had been…problematic. He didn't miss her as if he was missing part of himself. He missed what could have been without even knowing what that was.

He was going home now to another woman.

She might not still be there. She might have had her sleep and gone back to that appalling boarding house.

He'd fetch her back.

Um…no. It was none of his business where she was living.

But now half the hospital believed she was his long-term lover. And it was his business. He'd compromised her reputation. Maybe some kind of primitive instinct was kicking in, making him feel…

Dumb? Too chivalrous for words? He hadn't even had sex with her.

But the whole hospital thought he had, and he wasn't doing logic right now. He swung into the underground car park as Mrs Henderson was loading her buckets into the back of her cleaning van.

'Oh, Dr Williams, I'm so pleased you're home,' she said. 'I've been popping in to check on your young lady all afternoon and I didn't like to leave until you got home so I thought I'd do Dr Teo's spring cleaning. His place has been wanting a good going over for ever. But she's looking a little better. I gave her a nice boiled egg and she managed to eat most of it. She wanted to get dressed an hour ago but I said you wouldn't hear of it and if she tried I'd ring you. So she's gone back to sleep like a good girl. And she's lovely.' She beamed. 'Just lovely. I knew you'd find someone someday but I had no idea that you'd already found her... Lovely, lovely, lovely.'

He opened the door looking like a little boy expecting a bogeyman. If she wasn't so discombobulated, she would have laughed.

The last time she'd seen this man he'd been totally in control and she very much hadn't been. She still wasn't, but he looked like a man thrown overboard without a lifeline.

She shoved herself up on her pillows...on *his* pillows, she reminded herself...and tried to look dignified.

Gladys had helped her shower and change into her nightgown. It was quite a respectable nightgown. It wasn't respectable enough for greeting the man the whole hospital thought she'd slept with. Who'd held her paper bag.

'Thank you for the bed,' she said with as much dignity as she could muster. 'I'll get up now. I would have left sooner but Gladys was threatening strait-jackets.'

'And you didn't feel well enough?'

'There was that. It's a powerful little bug.'

'It hit most people harder than you.'

'Gee, that makes me feel better.'

'Sorry.' He wasn't sure where to take it from here, she thought. Neither was she.

'I will get up now,' she said.

'There's no need.'

Really? The thought of wriggling further down on these gorgeous pillows was almost irresistible—but this wasn't her bed. It was Luke Williams's bed.

'Gladys seems to think I'm your long-lost lover,' she managed. 'The sooner I'm out of here the better.'

'The whole hospital thinks you're my long-lost lover. It's not such a bad idea.'

She thought about that. Or she tried to think about it. Her brain was ever so fuzzily…well, fuzzy.

What he'd said was a very fuzzy statement.

'From whose point of view?' she said at last.

He ventured further into the room, looking suddenly businesslike. Professional. Doctor approaching patient with an action plan. 'From both of our points of view if you intend fulfilling your contract,' he said briskly. 'We were caught in a position that was less than dignified. If we were long-term lovers, the hospital grapevine would think it was funny and get over it. For a man and woman who met each other only hours before, it's like a great big neon light's appeared over your head saying "Condemn".'

There was much in that to think about. Condemn. It was a heavy word. Condemnation was how she was thinking of herself, in the fragments of time the gastro had given her to contemplate the matter.

But her self-image wasn't this man's problem. She'd held him. She'd wanted him as much as he'd wanted her. It was up to her to handle the consequences. 'I can handle a bit of condemnation,' she said, wondering if she could.

She thought of all the insults thrown in her direction since her father had died. She was her mother's daughter, therefore she was a Scarlet Woman by default. It had even ended her relationship with Charlie the Accountant, the man she'd dated for three years but who'd jibbed when expectations had turned to marriage.

'*Sorry, Lily, but I can't handle your reputation.*'

'*You mean my mother's reputation? My mother's behaviour makes me a whore, too?*' Her voice had risen...maybe more than she'd intended.

'*No but people look at you. I'm not sure I can handle that for the rest of our lives; people expecting you to turn out like your mother.*'

She'd thrown something at him. Something large and unwieldy that had just happened to be full of water and half-dead Christmas lilies. It had been a satisfactory moment in a very unsatisfactory interview, one that had left her feeling sullied. Mostly because she'd thought she'd loved Charlie and he'd loved her, and how could she have loved someone who thought her mother's reputation was more important than their relationship?

But her mother's reputation was important. It made a difference. Like her reputation was important now, if she was to continue working at the Harbour.

She was only at the Harbour for four weeks. She *could* handle this.

'I need a favour,' Luke said and sat on her bed.

*His bed.* She inched back on the pillows.

She'd held this man, why?

She knew why she'd held him. It had been the culmination of an appalling time, an appalling emotion. She'd felt a matching need in him and their mutual need had exploded.

There was no longer mutual need. They were strangers. There wasn't even attraction.

Um...yes, there was. He was rumpled after a long day at work. He'd hauled off his tie and his top shirt button was undone, revealing a hint of lean muscle underneath. His dark eyes were shadowed with weariness, and his five o'clock shadow was toe-curlingly sexy.

If he leaned forward and touched her...

She'd be out of here so fast he wouldn't see her go. What she was feeling scared her witless.

*She was not going to become her mother.*

What had he said? *I need a favour.*

'I don't owe you,' she said, cautiously. 'Or not very much. I mean…it was lovely that you helped me this morning, and you gave me a gorgeous bed to sleep in for the day, but—'

'I'd like you to sleep in it for a month.'

That was enough to take her breath away. A girl could be properly flummoxed with a statement like that.

'No,' she said.

'No?'

'It's a very nice bed,' she managed. 'But despite all evidence to the contrary, I keep myself nice.'

'I'm not propositioning you. I have a sofa bed in the living room. This apartment has two bathrooms. This bed can be yours for a month.'

'I have a bed of my own.'

'You're not going back to that doss house.'

'It might be a doss house,' she said with as much dignity as she could muster, 'but it's a prepaid doss house. It's okay. My bedroom's almost clean.'

'There are bedbugs.'

'Nonsense. I would have been bitten by now.'

For answer he tugged her arm forward, slid her

sleeve to her elbow and exposed a cluster of red welts. They both looked down at them. Irrefutable evidence. 'I saw these this morning,' he said. 'I rest my case.'

She stared down at the welts, perplexed. Bedbugs. She *had* been itchy, she thought. She'd just been too preoccupied to notice.

'Yikes,' she muttered. 'And double yikes. I'll buy insect spray.'

'You don't get rid of bedbugs with inspect spray. You get rid of them by moving out.'

'Not an option.'

'You have an option. Here.'

'I'm not in the market for a relationship,' she snapped.

'I told you, I have a very comfortable sofa bed. I'm not in the market for a relationship either.'

'I didn't even mean to kiss you.'

'Neither did I.'

They were glaring at each other. He was still holding her arm. A frisson of something…electricity?… was passing between.

She couldn't figure it out.

*Why had she kissed him?*

She wanted, quite fiercely, totally inexplicably, to do it again.

Get a grip, she told herself frantically. Even if her

body was operating at ten per cent capacity, she had to think.

She was so tired. She wanted to go back to sleep.

But a woman with no money, a woman who was dependent on her next pay cheque, *a woman like her*, couldn't sleep.

She glanced at the bedside clock. Seven-thirty. She was due back at the hospital at eight. She went to toss back the covers and then thought better of it. Her nightgown wasn't all that long. She didn't intend to make this situation more personal than it already was.

'I need to get to work,' she said, with as much dignity as she could muster. She glanced at her suitcase in the corner. 'Thank you for bringing my stuff. Would you mind giving me some privacy while I get dressed?'

'You're not getting dressed.'

'Says who?'

'Me. And there's no need. You're not required at work again until Monday.'

'Monday!' She gasped. 'Are you out of your mind? I've signed on for four weeks. If I don't go to work tonight, I've broken my contract. No pay. Do you know what that means?'

'The hospital's paying,' he said. 'Their barrier nursing clearly isn't working; they took out the controls too soon. The least they can do is pay you while you're sick. I've already organised it. Standard leave for this bug is four days—barrier nursing requires it. They don't want you back there before Monday but you'll be paid regardless.'

Whoa.

No work until Monday.

Four days with pay.

She could sink…

She couldn't sink. *She was in this man's bed.*

'You're looking paler every minute,' he said conversationally. 'You don't want to be sick again. Put your head down and sleep.'

'No!' It was practically a wail.

Why did he want her here? She was starting to feel like a white slave trader was standing at the end of her bed. *His bed.*

'I'm not holding you here against your will,' he said.

'Yes, you are.' She was having trouble making herself speak. 'If you won't let me get dressed…'

'Your baggage has been cavorting with bedbugs,' he said, prosaically. 'I'll take it down to the basement and fumigate it while you sleep.'

'But why?' It *was* a wail this time—she was reaching the point where the world was starting to blur.

He knew it. He took her hands in his before she

could resist, his strong fingers holding hers. The strength of him was infinitely...masculine. Infinitely seductive and infinitely comforting.

How long since someone had held her to comfort her?

He wasn't holding her to comfort her, she reminded herself, trying frantically to defuzz her thoughts. He was holding her to have his wicked way...although how he could want to have any sort of way with a woman who'd just stopped throwing up...

'We can help each other,' he said, quite gently, and she blinked and tried to think of something other than the feel of his hands holding hers. His gorgeous eyes; his gaze meeting hers, pure and strong. The strength of his jaw, the strong bone structure of his face, the shadow of a smile that was gentleness itself.

He'd make a gorgeous doctor, she thought. He *was* a gorgeous doctor.

'You're already helping me,' she muttered. 'Your housekeeper gave me an egg and toast soldiers.'

'Good for Gladys. I hope they helped.'

'I kept 'em down.'

'All the more reason why you should help me back. Stay here for a month.'

Her eyes weren't working properly. They kept blinking.

She was seeing him in soft focus. He was a beautiful man, she thought, and he was proposing that she stay with him for a month. Like a sheik and a desert princess.

Princesses didn't wear shabby nightgowns and smell of… She didn't want to think of what she smelled of, despite her shower. A night on duty, followed by gastro…

'I think you're weird,' she said. 'Go find a princess, instead of—'

'I'm not in the market for a princess,' he said, the gentleness fading a little. 'That's why I want you.'

'Pardon?'

He sighed, looked down at their linked hands and carefully disengaged. The gentle look became grim.

'I don't do relationships,' he said.

'I see that,' she said cautiously, casting a quick look round the sparse bedroom. This was such a male domain.

'But everyone in the hospital wants me to.'

This was important, she decided. She had to get to the other side of the fuzz. Figure out where reality and nonsense merged. 'You don't think that's just a wee bit egotistical?' she demanded, and his smile returned. It was a truly gorgeous smile.

His smile could make a girl's knees turn to putty— if a girl's knees weren't already putty.

'Sydney Harbour Hospital is gossip central,' he

said. 'Too much intense emotion, too many peo-ple working long hours, thrown together over and over… Everyone at the Harbour knows everyone else's business.'

'You're kidding,' she said faintly. 'I'd thought it'd be a huge, anonymous hospital.

'The Harbour?' He gave a hollow laugh. 'Anonymous is not us. Big or not, we're made up of individual teams. Everyone knows everyone else's business, sometimes I think right down to the jocks we wear. Actually, that may well be the literal truth; Mrs Henderson does my washing. This apartment block is home to at least half a dozen Harbour med-ics who also use Mrs Henderson, so I guess that's public knowledge as well. But since my wife died four years ago…'

'I'm sorry.'

'It's history,' he said harshly. 'But that's the prob-lem. The hospital, the grapevine, the whole gossip network has decided it's time for me to move on. Even my boss keeps pushing women at me.'

'Gee,' she said cautiously, her interest caught through the fuzz. 'So you're being besieged with women. That must be tough.'

'I've been married,' he said, maybe more harshly than he intended because he paused and softened his tone. 'What I mean is that I have no intention of going there again. I'd like everybody to lay off. You're in Sydney for a month?'

'Yes.'

'Then where are you going?'

'Brisbane?' It was the first place that came into her mind. It sounded a lot more fun than Lighthouse Cove.

'A month would give me head space,' he said. 'I've told them we've been in a relationship for a while.'

'You did that?' The fuzz was thickening.

'It protects your reputation.'

'Thank you.' She didn't feel like saying thank you. She felt…like she didn't know what to say.

He was being businesslike, a surgeon outlining an action plan. 'Apart from protecting your reputation, if we let everyone know what happened yesterday was the result of a long-term relationship, it helps me. I'm having four weeks with you and then you can go to Brisbane, you can do anything you like, but from my point of view you can be my absentee girlfriend for as long as I can carry it off. I'll tell them you need to care for an ailing mother or something similar. I can tell them we met on holiday a couple of years ago. That you come to the farm whenever you can. That I'm a very loyal lover. I'm thinking I might get two years out of this.'

'Two years…'

'Two years without matchmaking. Two years where I'm left alone.' He ran his fingers through his already rumpled hair and sighed. 'Believe me, in this hothouse, that's worth diamonds. And in return you get board for a month. You have to admit anything's better than that dump you were staying in. So…deal?'

The fuzz was everywhere, but his gaze was on her. Firm. Businesslike. Like what he was suggesting was reason itself. 'Platonic,' he said. 'No sex. Promise.'

'Of course there'd be no sex, but…' But her head was spinning. This was crazy. She'd be a pretend lover?

He was proposing an affair of convenience. No sex.

He really did have the most beautiful…pillows.

Oh, she was tired.

'You,' Luke said, with a certain amount of contrition, 'are wrecked. You need to sleep. I have another bathroom off the living room. We're independent. You sleep your bug away and then settle in for a month of businesslike contact. Would you like anything before you go to sleep?'

What was happening?

Sense was telling her to get out of this man's bed now; get out of his life.

If she did, she'd have to leave the pillows.

And… He'd just asked her if she'd like anything. What she wanted more than anything else in the world…

'Another cup of tea?' she murmured, figuring it couldn't hurt to ask.

He grinned. 'Your wish is my command.'

And five minutes later she was tucked up in his bed with a fresh cup of tea, plumped pillows, a spare blanket, the night settling in over the apartment. Five minutes later she was Luke Williams's Lover of Convenience.

# CHAPTER FIVE

SHE slept for almost twenty-four hours. Mrs Henderson popped in during the day with sympathy, tea, more eggs and toast soldiers, and some gentle probing.

Where had she come from? How long had she known 'our lovely Dr Williams'? Were they engaged?

She acted shy. She acted sleepy, which wasn't all that hard.

She slept.

The events of the last week had left her exhausted. In truth, the events of the last few years had left her exhausted.

She'd been her mother's keeper. It had been a full-time job.

Right now, her mother didn't know where she was and she couldn't contact her. When Lily left town she'd stopped at the headland overlooking the bay and tossed her cellphone as far as she could throw it.

If her mother had a drama—and she would certainly have a drama—Lily wouldn't even know about it.

She could guess.

Would the vicar stay with her? Would her mother be able to ride out the town's condemnation? Would her mother be able to operate the microwave?

Her father had treated her mother like a Dresden doll. He'd died when Lily had been twelve, and Lily had promised…

Enough.

She lay in Luke's bed with no cellphone, no way her mother could know where she was, and she felt… weightless.

She could even manage pretending to be Luke's lover for this luxury, she told herself. And Luke was serious about what he wanted. He'd slept in the living room, then carefully packed everything up before he'd left for work, checking and rechecking so Mrs Henderson would have no hint they'd slept apart.

Mrs Henderson supported her into the shower, clucked over her and helped her into a clean nightgown. Apparently Luke had gone through her baggage and given instructions that everything should be cleaned. She should be offended but she didn't have the energy. She lay in the vast bed on the crisp linen Mrs Henderson had insisted on changing. She gazed out of the windows at the glorious vista of Sydney Harbour.

Four days of nothing, nothing and nothing.

Apart from being Luke Williams's pretend lover.

'Wouldn't your mother want to know that you've been ill?' Mrs Henderson asked as she bustled back in to say goodbye for the night.

'No,' she said sleepily. 'I don't want to worry her.'

And her mother wasn't worrying *her*. Luke Williams's lover wouldn't have mother worries.

Luke William's lover didn't.


'So how long has this been going on? Why haven't we heard about her before this? Where have you been keeping her? And where is she now?'

To say he was besieged was an understatement.

Luke's Thursdays were always frantic—it was the day he did his kids' list, birth defects, procedures that took all his skill and emotion. Today he was doing graft work on Ruby May Ellington's left thigh. Ruby May was four years old. Born as a conjoined twin, her sister had died at birth. Her sister's death had meant there had been no hard ethical decisions to be made, but the surgery to separate them had been performed urgently. There'd been no time for preparation of excess skin flaps, and the grafting still was ongoing.

Luke had been working on this case when Hannah had died. The day she'd died, his team had saved Ruby's life.

The medical imperative tore a person in two. Like now, when he was concerned about the woman he'd left in his apartment. She was suffering from gastro but instinct told him it was more. She was too thin. Too tired. Too…shadowed.

She was running from something, he thought, but what?

He worked on, but the questions kept coming.

And they kept coming from the people around him.

Who was this Lily he'd kept so dark?

'Why didn't you tell us?' The head of paediatrics, Teo, a Samoan with a heart almost as big as his body, had been involved in Ruby's care from the beginning and, like Luke, he was willing the little girl a good outcome. It wasn't, however, deflecting him from hospital gossip. 'You've had this woman for how long?'

'That's none of your business.'

'Hey, this is the Harbour,' Teo said mildly. 'Everything's everyone's business. And now you've installed her in Kirribilli Views… You expect to keep her to yourself?'

'Until she's better, yes.'

'You have the next three days off, right?' With the procedure over, Luke was stripping off his theatre garb. Teo had hitched himself up onto the sinks and was regarding him thoughtfully.

'Yes.' What was coming?

He knew what was coming. Teo had a huge extended family and he treated the hospital as part of it. He shouldn't be a paediatrician, he should be a party organiser.

'I'm having a party on the beach on Saturday night,' Teo told him. 'My aunties are bringing food. You've knocked me back now one hundred and seventeen times...'

'A hundred and seventeen?'

'I've been counting,' Teo said. 'You disappear every time you have time off, and now we know why. But since you've introduced your Lily into the medical team, the least you can do is bring her along.'

His Lily? 'No.'

'No?'

Finn walked in and Teo turned to him. 'He's not co-operating,' he complained. 'Tell him letting us in on this lady is in his contract.'

'It's not,' Finn said shortly, and Luke glanced sharply at his boss. Was he in pain? His voice was tight, tense. Luke had seen a lot of pain in his professional life. There was something wrong.

'Leave him alone,' Finn snapped before Luke could get any further. 'He chose to flaunt his woman once, it doesn't mean he has to do it again.'

'I didn't…flaunt,' Luke said, and Teo grinned.

'Having it off in the on-call room? I'd call it flaunting. Bring her on Saturday. You're going to spend the whole weekend fending off visitors anyway. Word is Ginnie Allen's already figured out she's Lily's new best friend. She'll be knocking on the door asking for a cup of sugar right now. So…party it is.'

'Party it isn't,' Luke growled.

'Are you taking Mariette to Teo's party on Saturday?'

Finn Kennedy groaned. Surely as Surgical Director he should have privacy. He'd been back in his office for a whole two minutes and now Evie Lockheart was leaning on the doorjamb, surveying him with sardonic amusement.

'No.'

'No?' She raised her brows. 'Just as well. Everyone's tiptoeing around you but maybe someone ought to let you know David Blackmore, the new paediatric intern, is breaking his heart over Mariette.'

'What does that have to do with me?' The pain

in Finn's shoulder was driving him nuts and this woman was driving him nuts. She had no power in this hospital. She was one cog in a very big machine.

Her family money meant she could lean on the doorjamb and look…sardonic.

She also looked concerned. 'Is there something wrong with your arm?'

'No. Butt out.'

She butted, but only so far. 'Mariette's afraid to break things off with you because she's scared you'll sack David.'

'I won't sack David. And Mariette…'

'Has a reputation,' Evie said evenly. 'Which is why you're using her. You don't use women you can hurt. All I'm saying is that David's smitten and Mariette's worried enough to be not backing off from you for his sake. David might be the making of her. They say love cures all…'

'You're telling me this why?'

'Just so you know,' Evie said blithely. 'You're the ogre around this place. No one stands up to you.'

'Except you.'

'And Luke,' she said thoughtfully. 'There's another case in point. Love conquers all. He has a lady and he's taking her to the farm this weekend. I'm thinking we should change the quarantine rules so neither can come back to the hospital for a week. It wouldn't hurt to give them a push.'

'If you think I have time to waste…'

'On romance? I know you don't,' she said, and straightened. 'Just saying. Just going. Think about Mariette, though. She's a good kid at heart. And as for interfering with Luke's hot weekend—'

'I have no intention—'

'Excellent,' Evie said. 'I do like a man with no intentions.'

Every second Friday Luke had off. Every second Friday was tomorrow.

Luke's normal routine was to work for eleven days straight. He was happy to be rostered on public holidays, Christmas and Easter; in fact, he preferred it. But at the end of every two weeks he had three days off for the farm. For his sanity.

His farm was his place, his sanctuary, his solitude. Solitude? Lily?

The entire hospital now believed he was taking Lily there.

In the brief moments he'd had to himself since settling Lily into his apartment, he'd decided that he'd go to the farm as usual this weekend and that she'd stay where she was. Only now he'd started a lie.

Lily was deemed his long-term lover. He'd hardly go away to the farm the moment she arrived.

If he did, everyone at Kirribilli Views would know she was 'home alone', and what's worse, he wouldn't put it past them to drop in on Lily. To sympathise? To check on her for him?

He could see Teo dragging her to his party whether she willed it or not. The man's charm was legendary.

He didn't mind if Teo's charm was second to none, he told himself, but…

But his thoughts wouldn't go further than that one word.

One lie and a whole skein of deception had appeared.

Should they both stay here?

If he stayed here he'd be either pacing the hospital with nothing to do or he'd be pacing the apartment. With Lily.

So… Farm?

Would she come?

How did you persuade a stranger?

But she wasn't a stranger, he told himself grimly. She was his lover for a month.

Including farm time.

'John says you're going to the farm for the weekend. Oh, that's lovely. What's it like? He never tells us anything about it. He keeps everything so quiet. He's kept you so quiet.'

To say Lily was bewildered was putting it mildly. She'd opened the door, hoping the doorbell signalled a delivery or something equally innocuous, and an immaculately groomed woman with eyes darting everywhere swept right in.

'I'm Ginnie Allen. My husband's a clinical psychologist at the Harbour. We live in the apartment on the next floor up. I'm so happy to meet you. Oh, he's wicked, your Luke, fancy keeping you to himself. Has he told you Teo's having a party this weekend? Everyone's aching to meet you but he says you're going to the farm. He always goes to the farm. Surely you'd prefer the party?'

Lily clutched her bathrobe round her. Actually, it was Luke's bathrobe. Big and black and masculine, it fell to the floor and made an ungainly train.

She'd just woken. Her hair was ghastly. She was wearing no make-up. The woman before her looked like she'd just stepped out of *Sporting Vogue*.

To say she felt at a disadvantage was an understatement.

'And you're Lily...?' Ginnie waited for her to complete the name.

'Yes,' Lily said discouragingly, backing away

slightly. 'And I'm sorry, but I've been ill. If you could excuse me...'

'Oh, of course, you tuck yourself straight back into bed and we'll talk there. Would you like me to make us both a nice cup of tea?'

Tea had suddenly lost its appeal. 'I'd rather—'

'Coffee? No, dear, tea's much better. And toast? You need to keep your strength up if you're going to spend the whole weekend with Luke.'

'Hi, Ginnie.'

Luke. He stepped out of the apartment elevator in his suit and tie, with his briefcase in hand. Doctor coming home from work—to be greeted by the little woman in his bathrobe, and her new best friend, Ginnie.

'Luke!' Ginnie gave a crow of delight and hugged him before he had a chance to defend himself. 'Oh, wow, congratulations. You and Lily... I had no idea.'

'We're hardly announcing diamonds,' Lily said dryly, thinking she'd better nip this in the bud. 'Are you congratulating Luke on sharing his bathrobe?'

'I've no intention of sharing,' Luke said, and looked across Ginnie's head to smile at Lily.

And that smile...

Oh, that smile. She really was her mother's daughter, she thought, suddenly feeling frantic. If Luke had been the vicar...

She thought suddenly of the vicar, and for some stupid reason the thought made her want to chuckle. And wince. How could her mother fall for someone like the vicar when there were men like Luke in the world? Men who owned bathrobes like this. It must be cashmere, she thought. It was a caress all on its own.

His smile was a caress all on its own.

'I can't believe you're not coming to Teo's party,' Ginnie said reproachfully, letting Luke go and regarding him with huge disappointed eyes—and Luke's expression became a bit hunted.

*He always goes to the farm...* Lily wasn't sure what was happening here, but he didn't look the least bit like he wanted to go to any party. Well, neither did she. She didn't know what was going on but he'd lent her his bathrobe. He'd lent her his bed. Maybe she could afford to be generous.

*He always goes to the farm...*

'I'm not a city girl,' she told Ginnie. 'That's why I've only agreed to come and stay here for a month. That's why Luke and I can't be...as together as we'd like. But now I've been ill I'm—'

'Pining,' Luke finished for her, his smile still lurking. 'For the fjords.'

She cast him a look that was meant to put him in

his place. 'For fresh air,' she told him. 'For the smell of…sheep.'

'Horses,' Luke said.

It was becoming more difficult to be generous. Especially when he was still smiling.

'Especially for the smell of horses,' she amended. 'Eau de horse will cure me faster than anything.'

'You like farms?' Ginnie sounded incredulous.

'What's not to love?'

'Well, horses for a start,' Ginnie said, and shuddered. 'They bite.'

'Not my horses,' Luke said.

'Well, we wouldn't know,' Ginnie said, suddenly waspish. 'We've been practically next-door neighbours for four years and not one invite. You know we'd all love to see your farm. It's like you're keeping it a secret. It's like you've been keeping Lily secret.'

'It's because I know you hate horses,' Luke said blandly. 'Lily loves horses. She rides 'em to the manor born.'

Lily blinked. She loved horses?

Actually…she did.

A farm with horses. She thought suddenly…what was being proposed here? A couple of days on a farm with horses.

She might even put up with Luke Williams for that.

'Well, I think you should stay here,' Ginnie said crossly. 'Look at her.' She motioned to Lily-In-The-Bathrobe. 'She looks sick.'

'Gee, thanks.' But she *was* wobbly.

'My car's lovely,' Luke said reassuringly. 'Aston Martin, deep leather seats, pure luxury. And Lily even managed to protect them with her paper bag,' he told Ginnie. 'She's a heroine, my Lily. I'm thinking she can sleep all the way there.'

My Lily. The words hung.

This was getting out of hand, Lily thought, starting to feel hysterical. She'd agreed to this, why?

'How long have you guys been an item?' Ginnie demanded of Lily. '*Have* you been to his farm?'

Was now the time to back away? Lily wondered, hysteria growing. Pack and leave for Brisbane?

It'd have to be Brisbane. She couldn't go back to the Harbour after confessing this lie.

Luke had started the lie. Not her. She glanced at Luke, who glanced right back. Their eyes locked. His gaze was…almost a challenge?

*Are you about to tell the truth?*

Oh, for heaven's sake, why should she? she thought. What right did this nosey woman have to the truth?

Whatever, she decided. Go with the flow.

But maybe…not lie unless she had to?

'Merrylegs is my very favourite horse,' she said, tangentially.

'Merrylegs?' Ginnie blinked.

'She's given me years of joy,' she said and somehow, between Ginnie's prurient interest and Luke's bland withdrawal, she found herself remembering her first and one true love. 'She's beautiful. I know her so well she's almost part of me, and I wish I could be riding her now.'

'She's on Luke's farm?'

'All my horses are on my farm,' Luke said, sounding suddenly…wicked. 'Even though Merrylegs is Lily's favourite, all my horses are her horses.'

'How long have you two been an item?' Ginnie demanded.

'Years,' Luke said. 'Like Lily said.'

'How many years.'

'Three?' Luke said. 'I think. Isn't that right, dear?'

'Have you been staying on Luke's farm for three years?' Ginnie was almost speechless. 'That's not even a year after Hannah died.'

'I never met Hannah.' Lily faced Luke's wickedness head on. What had he called her? *Dear.* She lowered her voice, talking respectfully about her lover's deceased wife. 'Would Hannah have loved Merrylegs?' she asked Luke. 'Dear?'

'Hannah was more a cat person,' Luke said. The smile behind his eyes was challenging. Dangerous.

She rose to meet it. Challenging right back.

'You never talk to me about Hannah. I think you should.' She turned back to Ginnie. 'He never talks to me about Hannah,' she said, sounding aggrieved. 'I think our relationship would be better if he let it all out.'

'That's what John says,' Ginnie managed. 'So…'

'So, farm,' Lily said, trying hard to sound brisk when, in fact, all she wanted to do was retreat to Luke's bed and pull pillows over her head. 'We can pack pillows,' she told Luke. 'Your beautiful car might even be comfortable enough to sleep in. Mind, I'm more accustomed to the farm truck,' she confessed to Ginnie. 'But when in the city, act like a city girl, that's what I say. You might like to pack some more paper bags…*sweetheart*.'

'I guess we'd better start packing,' Luke said faintly. *'Darling.'*

'You start packing,' Lily said tartly, long-term-lover-like. 'I'm poorly. Ginnie, would you like to help? Maybe you could make me that toast you were offering?'

'Are you offering to make us dinner?' Luke asked, full of hope, and Ginnie backed out as if burned.

'I'll leave you to it. We'll miss you tomorrow night. Come back better, Lily. We'll have a lovely long chat on Monday.'

'I can't wait,' Lily muttered as Luke closed the door behind her. 'I just can't wait.'

To say the silence was loaded was an understatement. Luke closed the door carefully and then snibbed it, as if even now Ginnie might return.

Lily backed to the closest dining room chair and sat. Whatever energy she'd had had been spent.

'I'm thinking,' she said at last, trying hard to breathe so she didn't gasp, 'that communication seems to be lacking. So we're a couple. Congratulations are in order. We've been dating for years. We're about to leave on a romantic weekend to some farm I've never heard of.'

'Where you ride a horse called Merrylegs.' He seemed just as winded as she was. 'I believe two of us are playing this game.'

'It's not a game,' she snapped.

'I'm not laughing,' he said, and suddenly he wasn't. All this time he'd been holding his briefcase. Now he set it down, carefully, like it might explode.

That's what the atmosphere felt like, Lily thought. Loaded.

'I'm feeling a wee bit trapped,' she said, and hauled his bathrobe tighter round her.

'That's the part I don't understand.'

'What?'

'The trapped bit. You're an agency nurse. You could pack up and leave.'

'If I break my four-week contract.'

'I understand it'd make it hard to find another agency to take you. But there are other cities.'

'I don't have enough money to move to another city.'

'Would you like to tell me why you're in trouble?'

'No,' she said. She thought about it, thought about all the conclusions he might be jumping to, thought that maybe hiding any more conclusions wasn't a good idea. 'My mother's maxed out my credit card,' she said. 'She's done…well, let's just say savings I thought were in my account no longer are. She's taken a lover. We live in my tiny two-bedroom apartment and the walls are thin.'

'Ouch.'

'Her lover's the local vicar, husband of a prominent citizen, I'm a scarlet woman by association.'

'Double ouch.'

'Lighthouse Cove is too small.'

'I can see it might be.' He looked at her, not so much sympathetic as interested. Doctor inspecting patient. Looking at strange symptoms. 'So why not Adelaide? You trained there. You could get a job there.'

'And my mother would be on my doorstep within days, weeping, asking for money, needing support. Or worse, walking into the ward where I'm work-ing, weeping, asking for money, needing support. She's done it before and she'll do it again.'

'So Sydney.'

'For as long as I can manage,' she said wearily. 'For as long as I can get by until I need to go home and face the mess. I hadn't counted on running into a mess myself.' She sighed, and looked longingly at the bed. 'I'm really very tired.'

'You are,' he said, gently this time, as if the phy-sician had made his diagnosis and was moving to treatment phase. 'But this apartment block is almost an extension of the hospital. We'll be watched all weekend. The farm is best.'

'I don't want to move,' she admitted.

'It'd be better if I went to the farm and you stayed here,' he conceded. 'Only you'd get visitors and questions. At the farm you can sleep for three days straight. So what I suggest is that you sleep now for a couple of hours while I finish some patient notes, then I'll tuck you into my car and you can sleep all the way to Tarrawalla.'

'Tarrawalla?'

'It's where my elderly uncle lives,' he said. 'And the phantom Merrylegs.' He smiled. 'And the rest of my horses, all of which you ride like the wind.'

That smile…

She shouldn't.

Shouldn't what? Go to his farm? Sink into that smile?

No, she thought wearily, but her body was caving in.

'You're beat,' he said softly, and before she could guess his intention he lifted her and carried her to the bedroom.

'Put me…put me down…'

'Of course I will,' he said softly. 'I won't do anything you don't like, Lily Ellis. We've been unwise enough. Now's the time to be sensible.'

She didn't feel sensible. She felt…she felt…

Like Luke Williams was carrying her to his bed and there wasn't a thing she could do about it.

Travelling in Luke's car was almost like travelling in his arms. She lay back in her glorious leather seat, padded with pillows, ensconced in a soft cashmere blanket and felt…cherished.

'I feel like your ancient grandmother, being taken on a nicely padded outing,' she told him as he negotiated his way up into the hills north-west of Sydney. It was well past dusk. They were driving into the night and the passenger compartment was a pool of luxurious intimacy.

Luke's face was a focused profile against the moonlight shining through the driver's window. His face had such strength… He'd been hurt, Lily had decided after a few covert glances at him. Even if she hadn't known his wife had died, his face told her that. It looked…forbidding.

She was fighting an overwhelming urge to reach out and touch his hand on the steering-wheel, as a lover might, as a wife might.

Or an ancient grandmother ensconced in woolly cashmere.

'My grandmother wouldn't have been seen dead under a cashmere blanket,' he said, and she blinked.

'Past tense?' she said cautiously. 'Your grandma?'

'She died young; cirrhosis of the liver. Too much champagne.'

'I'm sorry.'

'There're worse ways to go. She was the society matriarch of Singapore.'

'Is that where your family live?'

'Yes.' Blunt and hard. The meaning was clear. Don't go there.

She wouldn't. But he had family. The thought jolted her. He'd seemed isolated.

He still seemed isolated.

And…he'd mentioned an uncle at the farm. Maybe it was time she learned more, even if she couldn't ask directly about his parents.

'So why aren't you in Singapore?' she ventured.

'I was sent to Sydney to boarding school when I was ten and I've stayed. A couple of visits home were enough for me, to be honest. My uncle did all the caring needed. He left Singapore when he was twenty as well, pleased to be shot of them.'

'So the Harbour is your de facto family,' she said thoughtfully. 'No wonder they matchmake.'

'They won't any more.'

'Because I'm the match.' She retreated under her cashmere and watched the car eat white lines. 'So after I leave…will you go back to being heartbroken?'

'I haven't decided.' He sounded amused. 'But I'm thinking I won't give up on you. You'll be heading into the sunset to find yourself and I'll be faithful for years, waiting hopelessly for you to return.'

'Wow,' she said. 'Like Miss Havisham, sitting in a pool of mouldy wedding dress.'

'That'll be me,' he said, sounding cheerful. 'So your family. One nutty mother. Who else?'

'Not a sausage.'

He shook his head. 'Everyone has a sausage.'

'Nope. My parents were both only children of elderly parents. My dad died when I was twelve. There's just been me and Mum ever since.'

'Cheap on birthday gifts,' he said, cautiously.

'Not so much. This year Mum's self-administered birthday gift was a trip to Paris for her and her vicar. She's disgusted because apparently I didn't have as much in my bank account as she thought. That's why she's still stuck in Lighthouse Cove, until her vicar finds the extra money—or her vicar gets tired of her.' She grimaced. 'It's a merry-go-round. I'll put more safeguards in place next time.'

'Next time… You'll go back?'

'I promised my dad I'd look after her and I will, but I need a break for a bit.'

'Of course,' Luke said, cheering up. 'For now you're my lover, or my ancient grandmother. But it doesn't matter. My farm's a haven Tom and I have created, a place with no obligations at all. My farm's for being whoever you like.'

Whoever she liked.

His lover or his grandmother?

Hmm.

She snuggled under the cashmere and thought, This could be a very long weekend.

# CHAPTER SIX

THE farmhouse was tiny, remote, perfect.

Lily gazed in awe at the moonlit valley; at the tiny house set high above a creek meandering through bushland. Mountains loomed in the background, blue-black in the moonlight.

A trail of smoke wisped from the chimney and a warm glow of light spread from the veranda.

'Who lives here?'

'I do.'

'But…the fire…the light…'

'My uncle lives in the big house. He likes his privacy. I bought the adjoining land so this is mine. Tom knows when I'm coming. He'll have brought in supplies, lit the fire, got the place warm.'

The night was warm and still. A mopoke was calling from the gums around the house. She could hear water rippling over stones, and frogs.

She climbed out of the car and the beauty of the place felt breathtaking. To have had the week she'd had, and then to find herself in a place like this…

Her eyes were suddenly filling with tears and she swiped them away with desperation. Luke was carting her suitcase up the steps. He stopped and looked back. 'What's wrong?'

'I… Nothing.'

'There are no padlocks here,' he said, mistaking her hesitation. 'I promise.'

I wouldn't mind if there were, if I got to stay here, she thought, filling her lungs with the gorgeous night air.

She could smell horses!

A million memories were crowding in. Her father, their farm, the horses she'd grown up with.

'When can I meet Merrylegs?' she managed, and made her feet head for the steps. All she wanted to do was stand and sniff the air.

'Merrylegs might be a bit hard to arrange,' he told her. He grinned. 'Though come to think of it, Tom told me we have a new colt since last time I was down. Merrylegs… Shall we take a look tomorrow and see if the name suits?'

'You'd name a colt for me?' She practically gasped.

'Think about it in the morning,' he said gently. 'You're shaking.'

How had he known? But she was. This stupid bug had left her so weak she was struggling not to cry.

She was out of control. But no. It was simply that

she wasn't under her own control. Luke was calling the shots and for the first time since her father had died someone had lifted responsibility from her shoulders.

She was back on a farm, without the burden of care.

She thought suddenly of the day of her father's death. Of him sitting at the kitchen table, a mass of bills around him, his face as bleak as death. 'Lily, if anything ever happens to me, you'll take care of your mother? Promise!'

She'd promised.

'Coming?' Luke said, and she looked up at this big, stern stranger, whose eyes were gentle but whose voice was inexorable. If she didn't move he was quite capable of striding down the steps, lifting her up and carrying her to bed.

The thought was…

Unwise. She made herself walk up the steps, into the beautiful little house, then up the stairs, into the made-up spare room and into bed.

She was asleep in an instant.

How could he sleep?

He didn't sleep much anyway. He lay staring into the night. So what was new?

Lily sleeping in his spare room was new.

He didn't invite people to this house. Hannah had made it beautiful, but he only used his bedroom and kitchen. He'd made the bed up because last year when the local stock and station agent's car had broken down a few miles from the house, he'd decided having the spare bed ready was sensible—but there was no question that this was his place.

To have Lily here was even more disconcerting than having her back at his apartment.

Why should it be disconcerting? She was a guest, a stranger in the next bedroom. A colleague. She was no different from the stock and station agent.

Or not.

Lily of the gaunt face. Lily who had been too thin even before the gastro. She seemed shadowed.

She needed this weekend. What harm was there in giving it to her? So what reason was there, then, to stay awake and be aware that she was just through the wall?

The whole hospital thought they were an item.

It'd been a spur of the moment deception but now…the thought seemed to be closing in on him. Deception or not, he didn't connect with people. Especially with complicated women.

Lily.

Hannah.

'Stand on your own two feet.' His father's voice seemed to boom from the darkness.

Luke's father and also his paternal grandfather were wealthy, foul-mouthed bullies. Luke's mother and grandmother were society gadflies, only interested in social standing. It was amazing they'd come together for long enough to produce children. Luke's father certainly hadn't wanted him. A son with a disfiguring birthmark had meant contempt from the day he was born.

What a family! His Uncle Tom had escaped Singapore as soon as he'd been old enough to emigrate, and Luke had been sent away at ten. Even though Tom had taken rough care of him since he'd arrived in Australia, Tom didn't seem like family. Neither uncle nor nephew knew what that was about.

Stupidly, Luke had tried family with Hannah. He'd spent four years thinking it might work; knowing it wouldn't. Then disaster.

Family was disaster. Emotional attachment was disaster.

'I have my farm and my medicine,' he told the darkness. 'That's enough.'

Whether Lily Ellis was his make-believe lover or not.

* * *

She woke and had to pinch herself to think she wasn't dreaming.

The bed was high, cast iron, the kind you'd expect in your grandmother's attic with a chamberpot underneath.

There was no chamberpot. There was a tiny bathroom right through the door. Lush towels hung from antique towel rails. Her patchwork quilt was gorgeous. The thick lemon carpet meshed beautifully with the soft blue walls.

This was no garret. This whole wee house was beautiful.

Had it been furnished by Hannah? Certainly there was a woman's touch—this was a far cry from the cool greys of Luke's city apartment.

She'd gone to sleep listening to mopokes and night owls.

Now there were kookaburras right by her window, their raucous laughter making her smile. How come they hadn't woken her until now?

She rolled over and reached for her watch. And practically yelped.

Ten o'clock in the morning? What the…?

Where was Luke?

She glared at her watch like it had betrayed her. What sort of guest was she? He'd think…he'd think…

Why worry? He already thought she was loose and fast; why not let him think she was a total slob? The damage had been done. She could sleep until midday.

Or not. Kookaburras. Sunlight on her coverlet. Smells, pure country.

It was Friday. She was here until Sunday; three whole days of farm.

She was out of bed, heading for the shower before she finished the thought.

They needed to be independent. Luke decided this at dawn, when he woke, headed to the kitchen for his standard eggs and bacon, and then hesitated and thought he should wait for Lily to wake.

No. She needed to sleep. Independence was the go. He needed to ride the boundaries, head over to the big house, spend a bit of time with Tom, do what he normally did on his first day here.

Lily needed to sleep for as long as her body required.

So he headed for Tom's but he made a phone call first. There was enough in what Lily had told him to think maybe some intervention might be needed. Without pushing the thought further, he called a lawyer mate in Adelaide. Then he left a note directing Lily to breakfast and headed out.

He found Tom, out with his dogs, eager to be doing things. Even though Tom was fiercely independent, he usually greeted Luke with a list of jobs the length of his arm. Today was fencing.

Excellent, Luke thought. Building fences, a man could get his thoughts together. Building fences, a man could forget about a woman with shadows, who'd melted into his arms and who'd…

No. Concentrate on fencing. He'd made the call to the lawyer. His conscience didn't require he worry any further.

Funny things, consciences. They had a will of their own.

The horse was young, Lily thought, watching him skittering toward her. Full grown. A gelding—he wasn't big enough, tough enough to be a stallion. He didn't look tough but he looked…bad? He pranced toward her and she could almost see challenge.

'Oh, you're beautiful,' she breathed as he came closer. She stood motionless against the fence, letting him assess her.

He was wearing a halter of tooled leather with a metal name-plate attached.

Glenfiddich.

He'd have been called Glenfiddich because he was

pure spirit, she thought, and couldn't resist reaching to touch.

Or not. The contact had him skittering back, rearing, then tearing round the paddock at full gallop. His coat gleamed in the morning sun, every muscle clearly delineated. He was glorying in his strength, in the morning, in the sheer joy of being alive.

Which was exactly how Lily was feeling. The sun was on her face. She was out of the city. For now her mother was the vicar's responsibility. She felt like she'd shed a too-tight skin.

'Did he rescue you as well?' she whispered, and the big horse dashed past her once, twice, and then paused. Slowed.

Decided to investigate.

She stayed absolutely still. He reached her and touched her cheek with his nose. He blew against her hair.

She swung onto the fence-rail, slowly, but he didn't shy away. He nuzzled her again, pushing his nose into her armpit.

She scratched him behind his ears and he threw back his head, backed away again, then tossed his head and came back for more.

He was a wild, beautiful thing.

She looked at the halter. Maybe not so wild.

Wildish.

He looked at the gate. So did she.

Dared she?

This was Luke's horse.

What had he said to Ginnie? *All my horses are her horses.*

There was soft rope by the gate; rope that could be looped as makeshift reins.

At twelve there wasn't a horse she couldn't ride. She'd helped her father break them. He'd taught her well.

She hadn't been on a horse since.

Oh, he was beautiful.

She slipped down from the rail and he started nudging her toward the gate.

She giggled and he shoved her in the chest. Hard. Like, hurry up, there's a world out there. Let's go.

Let's go…

They might find Luke. He had to be somewhere. On this horse she could go anywhere.

Not since she was twelve…

'Don't you dare throw me,' she told the nose shoving her toward the gate. 'My pride's at stake.'

Luke spent four hours with Tom. Thirty satisfactory fence posts later he decided he needed to check on his guest.

He swung himself up back onto Checkers, his favourite horse, elderly, big, black and docile, with the gorgeous white blaze that had given him his name. He needed to head back to the house and make some lunch. He'd take Lily for a gentle stroll over the more accessible places on the farm.

Or not. For suddenly he saw her, over the ridge, cantering down along the track toward them. And she was riding…Glenfiddich.

His breath caught in his throat. Glenfiddich was a half-broken yearling, as spirited as his namesake. Lily was riding him without a saddle, with the halter he always wore but no bridle or reins. She was using rope as reins.

The last time Luke had ridden Glenfiddich it had taken him an hour to settle him; to make him trustworthy. But here was Lily, her canter turning to gallop.

Was she crazy?

Even as the question hit, he was flying. Checkers was almost an extension of himself. He touched his flanks and his big horse flew toward Glenfiddich, veering at the last moment so Luke could grasp his halter. Glenfiddich tried to rear—of course he did— but Luke had him in a grip of iron. He swung off Checkers so he could take full control.

Glenfiddich objected—and so did Lily. 'What are

you doing with my horse?' Even though Glenfiddich had reared back she hadn't shifted on his back.

'He's not your horse,' he said through gritted teeth. He was fighting Lily for the rope-cum-reins. 'Give me the reins and get off. Tom,' he yelled to his uncle. 'Come and lift Lily off.'

'Does Lily want to be lifted off?' Tom asked mildly, strolling up to meet them and raising his battered hat to Lily. 'Seems to me she's got a pretty good seat. Pleased to meet you.'

'Get off the horse,' Luke snapped.

'So…you didn't mean what you said about me being free to ride whatever horse I liked?'

'He's not trained.' When he thought of what could have happened…a slip of a girl on a half-trained gelding…he felt sick.

'And I've forgotten my training as well,' Lily said happily. 'So we suit.'

'Get down!' His anger reverberated through the bush.

Lily stared at him in dismay and then slid expertly from Glenfiddich's back.

'I haven't hurt him.'

'You're lucky he didn't kill you.'

'I know horses.'

'Not this one. Of all the stupid, risk-taking behaviour… You're just like those kids, rollerblading over tallow.'

'You don't think you might just be overreacting?' she ventured.

'I didn't give you permission.' He had both horses in hand now, keeping them well clear of Lily. Glenfiddich was objecting but Luke was in no mood to let him show it.

'I believe you told Ginnie I rode every horse here,' Lily said, sounding angry herself now. 'I ate breakfast as your note said, but there were no instructions after breakfast. I inspected the creek, the home paddock, the horses close by, and then I thought I'd like to go further. Glendiddich asked me to ride him, so we've been exploring and here we are.' She smiled at Tom and carefully ignored Luke's fury. 'You must be Luke's Uncle Tom. I've very happy to meet you.'

*Glenfiddich asked me to ride him…*

He tried to take it in. This morning Glenfiddich had seemed to take his decision to ride Checkers as a personal insult. He'd kicked out as they'd left the paddock, and it was only because Checkers was an old and wise horse that there had been no damage.

To see Lily flying along the track toward him, bareback…

Gorgeous didn't begin to describe her, and fear didn't begin to describe how he'd felt.

'You're out of your mind, riding a strange horse,' he snapped.

'He's not a strange horse. We introduced ourselves before we got familiar.' She tilted her chin defiantly. 'Not like you and me.'

It almost defused his anger. A lesser man would have blushed. He almost did.

'Let the girl back up,' Tom said from behind them. 'She looks a picture on horseback.'

'I'll find you a quiet mare,' Luke snapped.

'Or a tractor?' Lily said, suddenly teasing. 'Tractors are safe but they're not nearly as much fun.'

'You're not here to have fun.'

Her smile died. 'Of course I'm not. I'd forgotten. Sorry.'

'Lunch,' he said, tugging the horses round to face the house.

'I guess we're not riding, then.'

'No. I'll find you a safe horse after lunch.'

Her smile died completely. 'It's okay. I guess I don't need to ride. I should have learned that a long time ago. Tom, are you joining us for lunch?'

Tom shook his head, but amazingly he looked almost tempted. 'No, but let the girl back on,' he told Luke.

'And have her break her neck? In your dreams.

I've had one woman die on me; there'll not be another.'

'Hey,' Lily said, startled. 'I'm not your woman.'

'Of course you're not,' he said shortly, and he led two horses along the track to the house without saying another word.

Luke worked with Tom again in the afternoon and Lily wandered the farm alone. She dropped by to chat—to Tom. She offered to help and when Luke said she should be resting she seemed rebuffed.

'She's a decent woman,' Tom said, eyeing Luke sideways. 'Good seat on her, too. Find her a horse.'

Luke had quiet horses but Lily's reaction had been blunt. 'I don't ride,' she'd said flatly. 'Forget it.'

He'd hurt her but he couldn't help it. He wasn't about to let her risk her neck.

But he did feel bad—and he had a foal she needed to see. Toward sunset, as Tom headed off to feed his cattle, Luke joined Lily on his veranda.

'I'm sorry I snapped,' he told her. 'I don't like people taking risks.'

'I wasn't taking risks,' she said mildly. 'But apology accepted.'

'I have something I need to show you.'

She looked at him, considering whether to take

the conflict further. She shrugged, moving on, and he was relieved.

What he had to show her should lighten the atmosphere, he decided, and led her over to Tom's home paddock to visit Zelda.

Zelda was a roan with soft white markings, a lovely gentle mare. The foal by her side was a tangle of spindly legs with his father's markings. Checkers's markings.

'Meet Zelda,' he told Lily, and Lily gazed at the foal in delight. 'And Merrylegs. Just named this morning.'

Tension was forgotten. 'He's beautiful,' she breathed. 'Is Checkers his dad?'

He nodded.

'A family,' she breathed. 'Mother, father, son. How lucky are you!'

'It's all the family I ever want.'

'Really?' she said, sounding startled. 'Why?'

Why?

He hadn't intended to say it. It had been a dumb thing to say.

So why had he said it?

Because she was too close.

Because she was too beautiful?

He'd hurt her today. He didn't intend to hurt her again.

He didn't intend to be hurt himself.

He forced himself to recall the day Hannah had died. She'd been unwell at breakfast but she'd thought it was the take-away meal she'd eaten the night before. She'd eaten too much of it, she'd snapped, because he hadn't arrived home in time to share.

'Ring me if you need me,' he'd said, knowing she was angry but not knowing what to do about it. He'd kissed her goodbye, intending to come home at lunchtime and check.

And then there'd been cojoined twins, one dead, one close to death, surgery impossible to delay. Fourteen hours in Theatre. At some stage he'd asked a nurse to ring and let Hannah know what was happening.

'The call went to your answering-machine,' the nurse had told him. 'I left a message.'

She must have gone out, he'd thought, relieved, and then all his thoughts had gone back to saving one little life.

While his wife and son had died.

So why had he said it? *It's all the family I ever want*. He watched Lily stroke Merrylegs's soft nose, he watched Lily fall under the spell of the tiny colt and he knew that he'd been warning himself.

'I don't do relationships,' he growled, and Lily cast him a look that held amusement.

'Good, then. Except pretend relationships. They're my favourite. So what will happen to Merrylegs? Will he be sold?'

'No.'

'So this farm…' she said cautiously. 'It makes a lot of money?'

He smiled at that, tension defusing. 'Not so much as you'd notice. We make a bit on the beef cattle.'

'I've seen your beef cattle,' she said. 'World's fattest beasts. I'm betting when they droop with age you move them into cattle nursing homes where they're pushed round in bath chairs until they die. And I've counted six horses I reckon are twenty years old or more. Plus you've bred Zelda with Checkers when anyone can see…'

'That's practical,' he told her. 'Checkers is getting too old to carry me and I'm used to a checkered blaze. It's like a flag on the antenna of your car how I pick my horse out in a crowd.'

She chuckled. The little colt nudged her chest and she hugged him. Zelda nudged her so she gave Zelda a hug for good measure.

'What a softie,' she murmured. 'You know your reputation around the hospital is cool and grumpy. And solitary.'

'That's the way I like it.'

'You could never be solitary with these guys.'

The sun was setting low in the west. Lily was stroking Zelda while the colt shoved her for his share of attention. The last rays of the sun were glinting on Lily's hair the soft evening breeze was making it ripple like silken waves.

Zelda was usually wary of strangers. She wasn't wary of Lily. She wanted to get closer. Touch.

Same with Luke. Maybe he could…

He raised a hand…and let it fall. No.

Talk about something else. Something to break the moment.

He had it. A reality check.

'I made some phone calls for you this morning,' he said. 'I went through university with a solicitor from Adelaide. He's made enquiries on your behalf.'

She straightened and stared. 'You…what?'

'Firstly the money. What your mother did was illegal. The bank wasn't authorised to transfer your money.'

'I didn't ask you—'

'I know,' he said. 'But it seemed…you're in such trouble.'

'That's my business.'

'But you can reclaim your money.'

'No,' she said, suddenly angry. 'I can't. Of course I know Mum's action was illegal but the bank won't refund money without wanting it back from some-

where. They'll have Mum arrested for fraud. Do you
think I want that?'

'If she's stolen—'

'She's my mum!'

'She's an adult. She's stolen—'

'Luke, my mum can't help herself,' she said, anger
giving way to weariness. 'She was indulged by dot-
ing parents and then by my dad. He adored her. All
men adore my mother,' she conceded. 'But apart
from my father, she never sticks to them. Dad com-
mitted suicide when I was twelve, lumbered with a
mountain of her debt. He made me promise to look
after her and I will. I know she can't help it. It's just
the way she is.' She took a deep breath. 'So, no, I
won't claim, and I won't have her arrested. I'll be
more careful in future. In a while I'll go home and
sort out the damage. But not…not yet.'

'You could go home now,' he said gently.

'I don't want to go home.' She said it with a vehemence that was startling. 'Mum's vicar will leave,'
she said, weary again. 'But not until my mother gets
tired of him, which won't be long. Meanwhile I'm
staying as far away as possible.'

'I'm sorry.'

'Yeah.' She gave him a shame-faced smile. 'I'm
sorry, too. You were trying to do good.'

'Gerald says he can get you damages.'

'Damages?'

'That's the second thing,' he said. 'According to Gerald, you were publicly slapped and dismissed without cause. Assault and public humiliation, with witnesses. The hospital board should pay damages.'

She thought about that. Her weariness and anger seemed to fade.

'The hospital board,' she said slowly, 'consists of five judgmental toads. I'm judged a bad lot by association. They only gave me the job because my qualifications beat every other applicant fourfold.' She considered a bit longer. 'Damages, eh?'

'It'd be a statement,' he said. 'A line in the sand.'

She considered a bit more. 'She did have cause,' she said. 'Vicar's wife discovering vicar with Mum.'

'Was that cause to hit you?'

'No.' She grinned, bouncing back. 'Does it cost to sue?'

'With the evidence as clear as it is, Gerald said one letter should do it, sent to the board with a promise to copy it to the press if damages aren't forthcoming. He reckons they'll be falling over themselves to limit fallout.'

'Ooh…'

'Do I have your permission to go ahead?'

She beamed and it was as if the sun had come out. 'Yes.'

'And the bank…'

'No.' Her humour faded. 'Mum's not going to jail on my account.'

'How long do promises last?' he said softly. 'A promise made by a twelve-year-old…'

'I know,' she said. 'It's ridiculous, but I loved my dad. I do this for him. Thank you for what you've done already but I won't take it further. My mum, my problem.'

He glanced at Zelda and at Merrylegs. Then he looked at Lily, at her expression of acceptance of a load that seemed almost too much to bear. He'd yelled at her, he thought, and he was sorry. 'Are you sure I can't organise you a quiet horse tomorrow?' he asked.

'Not Glenfiddich?'

'No.'

'Because?'

'I will not watch you take risks.'

'So don't watch.'

'Lily…'

'Okay, sorry,' she said, and held up her hands. 'You're trying to protect me. Thank you very much, but I don't need it.'

'You could enjoy a quieter ride.'

'I guess I could,' she said, but then managed a rueful smile. 'I know, it doesn't make sense, even to me, but I'd rather not. Not having been on Glenfiddich.' She took a deep breath. 'It's just… Luke, I don't want to be protected. For now I just want to be me.'

She seemed to wilt a bit after that. The gastro had knocked her, he thought, or maybe it was simply life that had knocked her. A crazy mother and a promise to the father she'd adored… She'd faced it alone since she was twelve.

He bullied her into toast and soup. She sat by the fire and gazed into the flames and he thought he shouldn't have let her out today. She should have stayed home by the fire. He should have stayed home with her.

*I don't want to be protected…*

What else was a man to do?

'Go to bed,' he said gently, and she cast him a look he couldn't understand.

'I like it by the fire.'

'You're exhausted.'

'Yes, but—

'But you don't sleep?'

'I slept last night.'

'Gastro would make anyone sleep. Is that why you signed up for night duty?' he asked. 'To keep the demons at bay?'

'I don't have demons.'

'I think…living with your mother must be nigh on impossible.'

'Like having your wife die? And the fear of facing that sort of tragedy again?'

'I'm not afraid.'

'I think you are. Wasn't that what today was all about?' She rose, a little unsteady on her feet, and he jumped up fast to steady her. He took her shoulders and held on.

He could draw her closer.

He didn't. He simply held.

A common bond—two nightmares?

It was enough to forge a friendship. This could be touching from mutual sympathy—but it felt much more than that.

The fire crackled in the grate, a sort of warning. That was a dumb thought, but right now anything was acting as a warning.

He should let her go.

He couldn't.

'Maybe you could curl up here and watch the flames while you go to sleep,' he suggested, and the tension around them escalated. Maybe he could stay here, too. The flames…the warmth…this woman.

He knew how this woman could make him feel. She could drive out his demons.

He couldn't make her safe. He knew she wouldn't let him.

'I will go to bed,' she said, and somehow she managed to step back from him.

'Count mopokes to go to sleep?' he suggested, and she smiled.

'Or frogs?'

'You don't have enough fingers and toes to count frogs.'

She chuckled and the desire to draw her close again was almost irresistible.

She stepped back fast, as if she felt it too.

'Goodnight,' she said.

He couldn't help it. He touched her hand, a featherlike touch, nothing more, but in that touch fire flared. It was contact that burned.

She tucked her hand behind her back. 'Luke...no.'

'No,' he said, and let his own hand fall.

They were pretend lovers. Nothing more.

'Goodnight,' she said again, gently, and she walked out of the door, closing it after her.

He stood staring at the closed door. Thinking, How much courage would it take?

Too much.

He wasn't tired. He headed out again, around the paddocks, following the line of the creek. How many times had he followed this route since Hannah had died?

It was different tonight. He was here because of Lily.

She touched such a chord… A woman keeping a promise at all costs. A woman of honour and intelligence and skill and laughter.

But…

The moment he'd seen her on Glenfiddich's back, he'd been hit with the knowledge that there was nothing he could do to protect her…

She'd guessed right. She'd known that his fear had been all about Hannah.

He looked over toward his uncle's house, where a solitary light burned on the veranda.

His uncle had learned the same hard lessons. He was like Luke.

They didn't do relationships. Not now. Not ever.

# CHAPTER SEVEN

LILY woke without the joy of the day before.

She could hear Luke moving downstairs. She heard Tom calling, dogs barking in the distance, and those dratted kookaburras.

Her stomach was cramping again. She'd talked to the doctor at home about the cramps. Tension, he'd said. Avoid stress.

Stress was sharing a house with a guy who was drop-dead gorgeous. Stress was playing pretend lovers with Luke.

She shouldn't have come. This was a stupid deception, designed to protect a reputation she didn't have and to add another level to Luke's armour, but by coming here a layer of her own armour had peeled away.

This farm…these horses…

Luke.

Okay, there was the problem. She was feeling what she had no right to be feeling.

He was feeling it too, she thought, but…

But she'd seen his panic when she'd been on

Glenfiddich, and his reaction had scared her. He'd yelled at her through fear. Shadows of a dead wife.

She was being dumb, she thought. This was an overreaction.

It was an overreaction because she was scared.

Because she was falling for Luke?

Maybe falling for anyone would be scary.

Growing up in her mother's dramatic shadow, she'd never thought of romance. Of falling in love. Drama, emotion were to be avoided at all costs. She knew the devastation they caused and it wasn't something she wanted.

Her relationship with Charlie had been like a comfortable pair of old socks. They'd been friends at school, they'd fallen into dating and they'd kept dating until suddenly Charlie had woken up one morning and realised he was heading for marriage with the daughter of the town tramp. When he'd cut her adrift she'd been hurt and angry, but she hadn't been heartbroken. Sometimes when she looked at romantic movies, seen friends marry, she'd felt like that part of her had simply not been formed. She'd been born without it.

Now… What she felt for Luke…

It was as if she knew him at some level she couldn't possibly understand.

She knew Luke's story—between Gladys and the

Harbour night shift she knew more than she'd ever need to know—but this went deeper than that. She'd instinctively joined the dots. Last night she'd said his fear for her was all about his dead wife and she knew it was. A lonely child, a tragic marriage… A man who walked alone.

He made her feel…

She didn't know how he made her feel. She felt… She felt…

She felt like she had cramps in her stomach, she decided. She felt like she needed to roll over in bed and put her pillows over her head, which was exactly what she did.

Avoid stress? Ha!

Luke worked with Tom, stringing wires between the fencing posts they'd put in the day before, then going on to rewire fences further along the creek.

All the time he worked he expected her to come. She didn't.

'You two still fighting?' Tom said at last.

'We're not fighting. She's had gastro. She overdid it yesterday. She should spend the day in bed.'

'Then why are you wiring fences?' Tom asked bluntly. 'With a woman like that in your bed.'

'She's in the guest bed.'

'More fool you. She's a good 'un.'

'There speaks an authority on all women,' Luke said. 'Curmudgeonly old bachelor that you are.'

'Had a woman once,' Tom said reflectively, astonishingly. 'Liseth.' He sighed. 'I thought maybe I had a chance, that our family hadn't stuffed me completely. But with parents like ours you don't rush into relationships. Anyway, I got drafted; Vietnam War. I was stupid enough to tell her to go out with other guys while I was away. I met her twenty years later, married to a car salesman. I walked into the office and she was there. She told me about her husband and her kids. All very polite. Then at the end when her husband was shifting the car she turned to me and exploded.

'I would have married you,' she said. 'In a heartbeat. Even if we'd only had those two months before you went overseas, it would have been enough.'

'Tom...' The vehemence of his uncle's voice shocked him.

'Yeah,' Tom said. 'I was a fool, like you were a fool with Hannah; but in your case the fool part wasn't one-sided. So we've made mistakes, do we have to keep making them? Enough. All I'm saying, boy, is life's short and she's a good 'un. Now let's get this wire done. And I want to talk to you about my arm. I damn near dropped the chainsaw on Friday. I reckon I might have tennis elbow.'

'Chainsaw elbow,' Luke said, and the old man grinned.

'You doctors have fancy names for everything.'

'Hi.'

The men turned and saw Lily at the edge of the clearing.

Uh-oh. How much of the conversation had she heard? Just the end, Luke hoped, though the silence in the bush meant sound travelled.

'I'm feeling better,' she said. 'I wanted to stretch my legs. And, no, Luke, I'm not about to ride another of your horses, even though I had to duck round Glenfiddich's paddock so he wouldn't see me. And I'm not here to interfere. I'll keep on walking.'

'Keep walking with Luke,' Tom growled. 'He's done enough for one day.'

'So must you if you have chainsaw elbow,' Lily said, teasing a smile from the old man.

'Nah, I'm fitter than the pair of you,' he retorted. 'You head off and do what a young feller and his lady ought to do.'

Luke looked at Lily and Lily looked at Luke, and Luke put down his tools.

What was it that a young feller and his lady ought to do?

\* \* \*

They walked slowly back to the house. She was walking a bit gingerly.

'Your tummy's okay?' he asked.

'Recovering nicely.' Her tone said not to go there.

'Rest this afternoon.'

'You should tell Tom to rest,' she said. 'Not that he will when you're around. He's lonely.'

'Tom—lonely!'

'He's like you,' she said softly. 'He drives people away. I met Patty Haigh up on your north boundary fence when I was walking...'

'Patty!' Patty was the cheerful next-door neighbour who cooked and cleaned for Tom. She was the mother of seven sons. She was always ready for a gossip—not that he and Tom gossiped.

'She worries about Tom,' Lily said.

'Tom's okay.'

'She doesn't like him being on his own.'

'Neither do I,' he said. 'That's why I bought adjoining land.'

'Why don't you commute?' she asked curiously. 'Patty says you can get to the Harbour in forty minutes from here.'

'An hour and a half at peak hour.'

'Since when do doctors travel at peak hour? You can fit your hours around traffic.'

'Tom doesn't want me here.'

'That's not what Patty says. He needs family.'

'He doesn't want family. Neither of us do.'

What did Lily know about Tom? he thought. Lonely? Tom was as fiercely independent as he was. But... Tom's revelation of moments ago had shaken him.

Regardless, it was nothing to do with Lily.

The chainsaw revved up behind them. He winced. He hated Tom using power tools when he wasn't here; it was a risk, the price they both paid for independence.

He blocked it out. Or tried to. He tried not to care.

'You want to go back and help?' Lily asked, looking concerned.

'He wouldn't thank me.'

'Like my mum doesn't thank me for caring,' she whispered. 'Sometimes you have to do what you have to do.'

'And sometimes you need to back off.'

'Like you have from everyone?'

'Butt out,' he said, trying to sound good humoured. If she was to pry into his personal life, the next four weeks would be endless.

'You made phone calls on my behalf,' she said mildly. 'Do you call that butting out?'

'That's...'

'Different,' she said cordially. 'You can butt into

my life, but I can't do the same in yours.' She glanced back along the track. 'That chainsaw…'

'He doesn't want us! He's vowed not to want anyone.'

'Like you?'

'I wouldn't know. Tom and I don't talk of it. What business is it of mine?'

'All your business if you love him.'

'Then you end up where you are with your mother.'

'Are you saying your uncle Tom is like my mother?'

'No, but…' He raked his hair. 'You can care too much. It leaves you open for hurt, like you've been hurt. It sounds to me like you should have backed off years ago.'

'Like you,' she said cordially. 'And Tom. Living in your emotion-free bubbles.'

'I like emotion-free bubbles.'

'Good for you,' she said, and smiled, and it was an entrancing smile. Enchanting. Beguiling. It made him want to…

Step right out of his emotion-free bubble.

It wasn't going to happen. *It was not.*

The chainsaw was roaring in the background.

They walked on in silence, using the noise as a silent excuse not to talk.

He was so aware of her, a slip of a girl with an enchanting smile, with judgment written all over her. And challenge.

He thought of Tom. Was she right? Was the old man finally admitting he needed people?

The chainsaw was biting through wood. It really wasn't safe, he conceded.

He had talked to Tom about it. Tom had told him where he could put his worries.

Suddenly the chainsaw's motor whined sharply, differently, rising in pitch as if it had been jerked free of wood. The wood was rotten. If Tom was pressing against solid wood and met rot…

Even as Luke thought it, the chainsaw motor cut out as it was meant to do the moment pressure was released from the hand hold.

And as the motor died…a scream.

Luke was running almost before his brain had processed the sounds.

They'd been replacing fence posts. The old ones had been hauled out and stacked.

Tom had balanced the first post against the pile, then started slicing it for firewood. Now he was sprawled on the damp grass, the chainsaw tossed beside him. The dogs were whimpering in fear.

A pool of bright scarlet was blooming out from Tom's leg.

Lily wasn't as fast as Luke. By the time she reached the clearing Luke had rolled Tom from curled and clutching his leg onto his back so he could see the damage.

In that one instant, she knew what had happened. He'd swiped the chainsaw downward. Maybe the wood was more rotten than he'd expected—maybe he hadn't needed as much pressure as he had exerted. For whatever reason the saw had sliced far further than he'd intended, smashing into his upper thigh.

He must have hit the femoral artery. It had to be cut, she thought with horror. There was no other explanation for this amount of blood.

Luke was searching for pressure points, one hand pressing, the other ripping at his shirt to try and get a wad, a tie, anything.

Her shirt was off in an instant, folded, handed to him. Then she grabbed Luke's sleeve and ripped with a strength she hadn't known she had. She ripped the sleeve right off, then ripped again from shoulder to cuff.

It gave them padding and a tie.

'Let me…let me…' Tom was gasping, trying to see.

'Lie still,' Luke snapped. There was no time for reassurance, not while the blood was pumping as it was. 'Tom, lie still. You've cut an artery and we have to stop it.'

'Bloody fool,' Tom muttered, and subsided.

His face was ashen.

So much blood.

The pad was doing nothing, no matter how hard Luke pressed. Lily was twisting the tie above the wound but making no difference at all to the blood flow. Already Tom was looking clammy, a sheen of cold sweat on his face.

He'd bleed out in minutes.

If they were back at the hospital they'd have tools to cut down, to find the artery and clamp it off. Here they had nothing.

'I can't locate it,' Luke snapped, and the agony in those words was desperate. 'Your hand's smaller. You try.'

It was a desperate request. He had nothing else to try.

He took the tie, while she shoved her fist into the wound, hard, as tight as it'd go. Was her hand small enough? She was searching for the source of the blood, pushing with a desperation born of terror.

Harder...

The blood welled around her fingers...and slowed.

Slowed more.

But in time?

She had to be in time.

'Hey, she's stopped the bleeding,' Luke told his uncle. Until now it had been impossible to disguise the panic. 'Lily's hit the spot. Don't you move, not a whisker.'

'I wouldn't dream of it,' Tom whispered. 'Oh, girl, I'm making you all mucky.'

'I love horses and I love nursing,' Lily told him, trying to match Luke's reassurance, trying to keep the strain from her voice, as if holding back blood like this was routine. Knowing how close to disaster they still were. 'I like a bit of muck.'

Tom tried to laugh but it didn't come off. He looked...

Like he could go into shock at any minute.

It was a real possibility.

Lily couldn't move. Her fist was a ball curled tight against damaged tissue, pressed hard against the pulsing artery. Somehow she'd hit the spot, somehow she'd blocked the blood supply. If she moved a fraction...

Luke was tightening the tourniquet with one hand, holding his phone in the other. Snapping details to an emergency service.

'Air ambulance, helicopter, code blue. GPS co-ordinates…' He lifted his uncle's phone from his pocket—a new model, Lily saw, and read the positional co-ordinates off. Thank goodness for technology. 'There's a clearing a hundred yards to the north. I'll secure it before you get here. If you can break the sound barrier I'd appreciate it. Move.'

He flicked the phone off.

There were sheets of paper-bark hanging from the massive gums along the river. While Tom—and Lily—stayed motionless Luke hauled a dozen of the soft bark sheets, folded them into a wedge and manoeuvered them with extraordinary care underneath Tom's hips and legs. He had to be careful; there was no way he was interfering with Lily's position. But it had to be done. Any available blood needed to flow to Tom's head and not to his lower limbs. His hips had to be higher than his heart.

Done. He twisted the shirt tighter around Tom's thigh and Tom grunted in pain.

'I have emergency gear in the car,' he told Lily. 'Catheters. Saline. Morphine.'

'Then why are you here?' She was impressed by how calm she sounded. Luke needed to get an IV catheter in now, if not sooner. If Tom's veins collapsed, resuscitation would no longer be possible.

They both knew that point was close.

'I'm going.' Luke sounded agonised. He'd hate to leave but he couldn't stay. He touched his uncle's face, then he touched Lily on the shoulder—a feather-light brush.

Then he was gone.

They were the longest minutes of Lily's life, keeping pressure on the wound, praying Tom's condition wouldn't worsen. Trying not to let Tom see she was terrified.

The dogs, Border collies, lay and watched and she sensed their fear as well.

'I hope Luke can run,' she ventured, and Tom tried a smile.

'Like the wind,' he whispered. 'He spent half his childhood running on this farm. Most weekends. All his school holidays. Ran all over this farm.'

'Did he never go back to Singapore?'

'Parents sent him to boarding school to get rid of him,' Tom muttered. 'He had a ruddy big birthmark on his face. His parents hated looking at it. My brother was too mean to get it fixed, though. Told the kid it was character building but in truth he was fixated on money. Like that bloody wife of his…'

He broke off and gasped and Lily wished she could hug him, wished she could move. Selfishly she also wished she could alleviate the pins and needles in her hips.

She could do nothing.

They were totally dependent on Luke. He needed to fetch equipment. He needed to check for a safe place for the helicopter to land. It was maybe a ten-minute run back to the house. Ten minutes there, ten minutes back, time to get land cleared…

All she could do was sit.

It was killing her. It *was* killing Tom. With every moment his chances grew slimmer.

Then, before she imagined it was possible, she heard the roar of a motor revving through the trees, crashing…and Luke's Aston Martin broke into the clearing, bush-bashing like he was driving an ancient SUV rather than a sports car. No matter, he was here. He was out of the car almost before it stopped, hauling his bag with him.

'Tom…' She heard the catch in his breath, knew how terrified he'd been of what he'd find.

'We're fine,' Lily said quickly. 'And we always knew Aston Martins were offroaders.'

He managed a fleeting grin as he hauled a catheter from his bag.

'You drove that thing through the bush?' Tom

gasped, and Luke's smile became genuine. Luke would have run thinking the worst, Lily thought. He'd have known that if Tom had gone into cardiac arrest while he was gone there'd have been nothing she could do—not when taking her hands from the pressure point meant blood loss would resume.

But now…

Luke was inserting a catheter. He had IV fluids! Not blood product, she thought, that'd be too much to hope from most emergency kits, but he had saline, and any fluid was a lifesaver.

Could be a lifesaver.

Please.

The catheter was inserted in seconds. An IV line was set up.

'There's morphine going in, Tom,' Luke said. 'Any minute now you can stop gritting your teeth.'

'I'm not gritting my teeth,' Tom said, indignant. 'Or not very much.'

Lily let out her breath, not knowing until then that she'd been holding it. There was a chance…

'I'm releasing the tourniquet for a moment,' Luke said. 'I'm not saving you only to lose that leg. You might want to grit those teeth.'

'Pansies grit teeth,' Tom said, though the expression on his face said the pain was bad. 'Me and Lily aren't pansies.'

'You and Lily can face the world with your heads held high,' Luke said. 'Pansies? I don't think so. Heroes, both of you.'

'It's our Lily. I'm just lying here thinking of England.'

'Well, think of England a while longer,' Tom said. 'I need to get the paddock cleared for the chopper. Harbour Hospital, here we come.'

'Hey, we might even be in time for Teo's party,' Lily managed, desperately striving for lightness. 'Tom, there's a party on the beach tonight. You want to get stitched up and come?' They all knew how impossible it was, but the thought was a good one.

Tom groaned. 'Parties,' he whispered, trying to sound withering. 'Mind, if alcohol's involved, I wouldn't mind a wee drop.'

'Neither would I,' Lily said, with meaning. 'And not so wee at that.'

The helicopter arrived soon after with a team of paramedics from the Harbour who knew Luke by name.

Jack Stephens, trauma specialist, was in charge. The team must have understood the call was deadly serious to have sent a physician of Jack's standing. In her two nights in the Harbour Lily already knew this guy's reputation and he was with a team who were just as awesome. They worked with competence and speed, and a light-hearted banter that made Tom relax as nothing else could.

'For years we've been trying to wangle an invitation to see the place where Luke hides out,' Jack told Tom as he replaced IV saline with blood product and set up another line in case of need, then checked Lily's position and placed a hand on her shoulder—a silent message not to move. 'Thanks for organising it. I guess you're not quite up to guided tours.'

'Maybe another time?' Tom said weakly, and Luke gripped his hand and held.

'Don't agree to anything,' he urged. 'This guy's a freeloader from way back. He'll have conned you into bed and breakfast in no time.'

'I'm guessing it's you who needs the bed and breakfast,' Jack told Tom. 'Let's get you back to the Harbour.' He cast an uncertain look at Lily, looking closer at where her hand lay. 'And I'm thinking we're taking Lily as well. You've got a pulsing artery there, Tom. Lily has her hand on exactly the right spot and it's hard to reach. If we try to clamp it here we risk more blood being spilled and you've made enough of a mess already. Lily, can you stay where you are while we work around you?'

Luke made an involuntary protest. To have Lily hold that position during transfer…

But it was the only way. Where she was now, not only was she holding the blood flow back but somehow she'd lucked onto a position where a tiny amount of blood was seeping through to Tom's foot. To take Lily away, to slice down, to tie off the artery, keeping the blood supply to the foot uncompromised...

It had to be done in a well-equipped theatre to give Tom any chance of keeping his leg, as well as his life.

'I've never ridden in a helicopter,' Lily said. 'Cool.'

She was amazing, he thought. She was as pale as a ghost, still shaken by gastro. Her jeans were blood-soaked and she was only wearing a bra on top. She wasn't moving. She knew what needed to be done and she was doing it.

'We can't fit you in as well,' Jack told him, and grinned at the look on Luke's face. 'This is cool indeed. Our team has the whole ride back to grill Lily and Tom about our Dr Williams's secret love life and secret farm life. The hospital's been bursting with questions since Wednesday. Now, you, Luke Williams, can butt out and calmly drive your poncy little car back to the Harbour while we do our interrogation as we ride in real transport. We'll do our best to save your uncle's leg while we're at it. By the way, you might want to stop and collect pyjamas for your uncle on your way. That'll give us more time to interrogate. Okay, guys, let's move.'

The Aston Martin, loaded now with two subdued dogs, took a lot more time getting back to the road than it had taken getting to his uncle.

He'd hit a couple of small trees, bush-bashing in his desperation to get back to Tom and Lily. His front fender was bent. He stopped at Tom's house and had to do a bit of rebending in order to protect the wheel. He didn't want any hold-ups on the way back to hospital.

He was thumping the fender one last time when his neighbour Patty arrived, looking scared.

'I saw the chopper,' she said. 'From the Harbour. What's happened?'

He told her, and she offered to pack Tom's bag while he got the car sorted.

'I'll take care of the dogs and the rest of the place as well,' she said. 'Tell him Bill and I will drop in and see him as soon as he's well enough for visitors.'

'He won't want—'

'He always says he doesn't want,' she said. 'But what men say and what men mean are different things. Like telling me he doesn't need me bringing him casseroles and pies. Like telling me he doesn't want you living here. He's a lying hound but he's *our* lying hound so we'd be grateful to have him home safe and sound.'

He left her, but her words stayed with him.

*What men say and what men mean are different things...*

If he and Lily hadn't been there today...

Tom couldn't stay on the farm any more. Not alone. They'd have to find him a live-in housekeeper.

He'd hate it.

Could *he* finally decide to commute?

Tom would hate that, too. He'd put up with him as a kid, because he'd felt sorry for him. He tolerated Luke owning the place next door and he appreciated his help, but essentially he was a loner.

Tom didn't want Luke close, like Luke didn't want anyone close.

Anyone like Lily.

His thoughts should have only been on Tom. Instead they kept drifting to a shadowed girl with bloodstained clothing and a courage that defied belief.

Riding Glenfiddich yesterday.

Holding Tom today.

Facing down the gossip of the Harbour.

Coping with a mother who sounded like a nightmare.

Wasn't he supposed to be worrying about Tom?

He was feeling sick about Tom. No matter that he was in good hands, there was still a chance…

Don't go there.

He was going as fast as the speed limit and a slightly buckled Aston Martin allowed. The chopper would be back at the Harbour by now. Jack and his team would be doing their utmost to save Tom.

Would they have released Lily?

She'd go into Theatre with them, he thought. They'd leave her hand in position while Tom was anaesthetised, while they put every tool in place so they could work with speed to cut down, clamp, tie off, without compromising what little was left of the leg's blood supply.

Then Lily could step away.

He needed to be there when she stepped away.

How fast could he make this car go? Not fast enough.

He hit the phone. Evie.

'He's here and he's still with us,' Evie said before he could say a word. 'Jack's taken him straight through into Theatre. He had everyone lined up before he got here. Finn's supervising. Judy's on her way. You have the best surgical team the Harbour can provide.'

'Lily…'

'Lily still has her hand in place. We're not shifting her until we're sure we can get in fast enough.'

'Can you be there when she's no longer needed?'

'I'll have one of the nurses—'

'I want you, Evie,' he snapped. 'I don't ask favours, but I'm asking for one now. She's had gastro. I'm worried about her as well. It'll be twenty minutes before I get there. Be there for Lily for me.'

'If it means that much…'

'It means that much,'

'Well, well,' Evie said gently. 'And I thought it was mostly gossip. You really do care. Don't worry, Luke, of course I'll be there.'

# CHAPTER EIGHT

LILY woke and someone was holding her hand.

That someone was Luke.

She blinked but she wasn't dreaming. Luke Williams was leaning over, smiling, and he was definitely holding her hand. Her fingers were on the coverlet. His were entwined with hers.

Sunlight was streaming in the window, or rather the rays of a tangerine sunset. She was warm and cosseted and...

*Luke Williams was holding her hand.*

'Hey, sleepyhead,' he said softly, and his hold on her hand tightened. 'I thought you might be intending to sleep until morning. Mind, you have the right.'

His voice was low and husky, tense with emotion. His face was drawn.

It definitely wasn't a dream. The day's events flooded back and with it, dread.

'Tom...'

'Tom's fine,' he said, and he didn't release her hand by a fraction. 'Judy Nerolin, our senior vascular surgeon, has decreed his leg will be okay and no one argues with Judy. He's out of Theatre. He's still in Intensive Care but all the signs are that he'll make it and even make it with his leg intact. Thanks to the team from the Harbour—and one amazing nurse. One nurse called Lily.'

'Hey, I didn't do anything,' she said sleepily. 'Except put my fist in a hole. Like the boy with his thumb in the dyke in Holland. Highly skilled stuff.'

'You fainted,' he said ruefully.

'But not until Judy took over,' she said with pride. 'I told myself I couldn't and I didn't.'

'You mean you knew you were going to faint.'

'By the time they rolled us into Theatre I was feeling a bit light-headed,' she admitted. 'But then Dr Lockheart brought me up to this cool bedroom.'

It was indeed a cool bedroom. This suite was for the Harbour's wealthiest, most influential patients. It was more a suite of rooms than a bedroom.

Dr Evie Lockheart's family were principal bene-factors of this hospital. They were Sydney's an-swer to royalty and what royalty decreed, royalty received.

Royalty had obviously decreed Lily deserved this bedroom and Luke wasn't arguing.

He should pull his hand away. He didn't.

He'd been sitting here for the last ten minutes,

watching her sleep. Her curls were sprawled over the pillows. She was stained and battered.

She'd fought and she'd won. For Tom.

He wasn't supposed to feel like this. Had Tom taught him nothing?

He remembered the first time Tom had come to collect him from boarding school. It had been his first week there, aged all of ten, and to say it had been ghastly was an understatement.

'You teach yourself you don't need anyone,' Tom had growled. 'You grow up tough and you stay tough.'

That's what his father had said when he refused to pay for the removal of the birthmark. 'It'll make you tough.'

He'd sent him away, though. Tom had been raised with the same philosophy, had learned the hard way how it worked, but he'd bent the rules.

He'd cared for Luke.

Luke now cared for Tom in a way he hadn't realised. He'd thought the only person he'd ever fallen in love with was Hannah. It wasn't true, though. Seeing Tom's life hang so precariously, he knew he was exposed to pain all over again. And now this slip of a girl, who'd hung on for over an hour, knowing if she moved a sliver of an inch they'd lose…

It was her bravery that moved him, he told himself, not the woman herself, but he knew it was much more.

He thought of her suddenly on Glenfiddich, and the dread surfaced. He thought of Tom and the chainsaw.

When Luke had been fifteen Tom had been bitten by a snake. He'd recovered but Luke remembered thinking, If he dies I have no one.

'Don't watch me if you're worried,' Tom had snapped, and Luke had been trying not to watch ever since.

It wasn't working.

'I'm sorry I overreacted about Glenfiddich,' he said. 'Give me another six months to train him and you can ride him all you like.'

'All by myself?' she demanded, mock-awed. 'Will you buy me a stepladder to climb up with?'

'Lily...'

'No, it's a very generous offer,' she whispered. 'Sorry. I should have asked before I rode him.'

'And I should have stayed home with you.'

'Watching me in case I did anything dangerous?' she asked, her eyes clouding. 'Is that the problem? Is that why you can't stay with Tom—because you can't bear that he does dangerous things whether you're watching or not?'

'That's deep,' he said, and tried a smile. 'Have you been talking to John Allen?'

'I don't need a psychologist to figure out something's wrong. Luke, go away.'

But her hand didn't disengage from his.

'You want me to leave?'

'I need to take a shower. I'm fine. Fainting was just a reaction. Even the strongest woman might have been tempted to faint, so a wuss like me...'

She was laughing again! After all she'd been through...

She was enchanting.

Love...

Whoa. Step away now, he told himself.

Don't watch.

He could no sooner not watch than fly.

'I could help you shower.'

'In your dreams, Dr Williams.' She grinned. 'Since when do plastic surgeons shower patients?'

'Three nights ago a very bossy nurse said I should do just that.'

Her lips twitched. 'That was some cheek.'

'I think you're wonderful.'

The laughter in her eyes faded. She met his look square on. 'Luke, don't.'

'Don't?'

'You want me to share your apartment for a month. That's not going to work if you make me feel…'

She didn't finish but he knew what the words were.

Their eyes locked, and something was happening. A link, a connection, growing stronger every second.

He wanted to lean forward. He wanted to take her in his arms and…

The door opened and Lily flinched. He pulled back, not sure whether to be glad or sorry.

No. He was definitely sorry.

Evie Lockheart opened the door with caution. She smiled as she saw him, and she smiled even wider when she saw Lily was awake.

'Hey,' she said. 'We were worried about you. Nurses collapsing in Theatre does our safety record no good at all.'

Lily smiled back, looking embarrassed. 'I'm sorry.'

'No need to be sorry. The whole hospital's in awe of what you did. Saving Luke's uncle…' She glanced at Luke and grinned. 'And the hosital's on fire with the story. In one fell swoop we've met your lady, your uncle and your farm. Where's your precious privacy now?'

'Shot to pieces,' Luke admitted.

But Evie was focusing on Lily. 'How are you feeling?'

'Fine.'

'You don't look fine.'

'Because I'm covered in blood,' Lily said with dignity. 'If I could have a shower…'

'I'll send a nurse to help you.'

'I don't need—'

'Tell me what you need when I'm interested,' Evie retorted. She elbowed Luke out of the way and felt Lily's pulse.

'She's had gastro,' Luke reminded her. 'The plan was for her to rest this weekend.'

'Yeah, like that worked,' Evie said dryly, assessing Lily with professional concern. 'You're too thin.'

'I'm always thin.'

'No other symptoms?'

Lily hauled her hand away and tucked it under the covers. 'I'm okay. Honestly, gastro and this afternoon would make anyone faint.'

'I guess.' Evie turned to Luke. 'Look after her.'

'I will.' And he surprised himself by how much he meant it. 'She won't let me help her shower, though,' he complained, and Evie grinned.

'Good. She needs to rest.'

'I wouldn't…' He practically blushed.

'You're male,' she said darkly. 'Of course you would. I'm with Lily. I'll send in a nurse.'

'I don't need help,' Lily said.

'You'll take it. Shower and back to bed for the night.'

'I'm going home,' Lily said, and then hesitated. *Home.* The word had connotations for them both.

But Evie was being efficient. It was up to him to be the same. 'I'll collect you as soon as you're clean,' he said. 'I'm going to check on Tom but I'll be back in half an hour, Lily. I'll bring the car to the discharge area.'

'I'm not a patient.'

'No,' Evie said. 'You're a heroine. The Harbour takes a while to accept people as its own, but what you've done this afternoon…you're now one of us, like it or not. We might gossip, we might be in your face, but we do look after our own. Luke takes you home or you stay here, like it or not.'

'Fine,' she said helplessly. 'I mean, thank you.'

'You're welcome,' Evie said, and grabbed Luke's arm and steered him out of the room. 'Expect a nurse. Luke, let's leave the lady to get on with what she needs to do.'

The nurse took a while to come. That was fine by Lily. She watched the sun set over the distant harbour and she felt as if she was floating.

Luke was taking her home.

She could still feel the pressure of his fingers on hers. He didn't know his own strength, she thought.

He'd almost kissed her.

She'd wanted him to.

Which was really dumb. It must be because she was still tired and overwrought. Today—or, to be honest, the last few days—had taken it out of her.

Her stomach still hurt. Stress?

Maybe she should have said something to Evie.

No. She simply needed to give herself time to get over the gastro. To get over today. And more, she needed to *stop stressing*.

How could a girl do that when she was heading to Luke's apartment? What had she got herself into?

She sighed and closed her eyes. At least her mother wasn't here, and with that thought came more. How was her mother coping?

Her father's voice… 'You will look after her?'

She was so tired.

A young nurse peeped round the door. 'Dr Lockheart said you'd like help to shower. Dr Williams has given me a bag with some clothes. Are you up to showering now? Dr Lockheart says if you'd like to have another sleep first then Dr Williams will wait.'

'No,' she said, pushing herself upright. Reluctantly. 'No, it's okay. I need to go home.'

Wherever home was.

Home with Luke?

'So why's she looking like she's been hit by a train?'

To say Evie was blunt was an understatement. She said things as she saw them.

'She had gastro.'

'You and I both know gastro doesn't make you look like that. There's no underlying medical problem? She went out like a light in Theatre. She scared the hell out of Judy.'

'She's been under strain.'

'Because of your relationship?'

'Will you butt out?' He turned to face her head on. Finn had labelled her Princess Evie. The staff still called her that, not to her face but as a gentle reminder to themselves of the power she wielded. Evie was one doctor among many, but her family money meant she was unsackable. Her grandfather had brought her in here when she was tiny, she'd practically lived in his office and she thought of the place as home.

So this hospital was her home and she didn't like mess. She was trying to tidy Lily up, he thought. Pigeonhole her. Figure exactly where she fitted.

'She almost looks abused,' Evie said conversationally, and he practically spluttered.

'You're accusing me of abusing...*my girlfriend*?' It took him a while to find the last two words but he managed it.

'I'm not saying anything of the kind,' Evie said. 'That's why I'm asking. I said almost. What other explanation is there?'

He groaned inwardly. There was no way she'd leave this now; no way she'd stop pestering him. If he didn't give her what she wanted then he had no doubt she'd march right back and ask Lily. If she thought a woman was in trouble...

She might be Princess Evie, but she had courage and honour.

Almost as much as Lily?

He had to give her the truth, he thought, or as much as he needed to divulge to get her off both their backs.

'Lily's having trouble with her mother,' he said. 'Major trouble.'

'Illness?'

'Her mother's stolen her savings and has taken up with the local vicar. And if you repeat that to a soul I don't care who your family is, I'll hang you out to dry. I imagine Lily would kill me if I told anyone.'

Evie stared at him, stunned. 'All her savings...'

'Yep.'

'So that's why she's finally staying with you. Oh, the poor girl.'

'I'm fixing it,' he said heavily.

'You're fixing it?'

'As much as she'll let me.'

'You?' she said, and he wondered what exactly the staff did think of him.

'Leave it,' he said, and her face creased into a smile.

'Our Luke, fixing it,' she said happily. 'How about that? Falling for a woman with problems.'

He wasn't.

Or wait…maybe he was.

He needed to get things in perspective.

He wasn't sure what perspective was.

'Luke, while you're in fixing mode…' Evie said

And he thought, Uh-oh, here we go. He did not have this kind of conversation with Evie. He didn't have this kind of conversation with anyone.

Did Evie suddenly think he'd changed?

'It's Finn,' she said. 'I'm worried.'

Here was another jolt. Evie wasn't a worrier; she was a brisk, efficient doctor with the weight of the Lockheart fortune behind her.

Finn.

The niggle of worry he'd been feeling about his

friend surfaced again, and turned into something more substantial.

But this was Finn Kennedy they were talking about, and no matter how much money Evie's family had, he wouldn't thank Luke for crossing boundaries. A junior doctor was talking to him about his boss. 'I don't think he'd thank you for worrying about him,' he said dryly.

'You're his friend,' Evie snapped.

Was he? Finn didn't do friends. Still… He'd been there when Finn had been released from the army. He'd spent time with him whether Finn wanted him or not. The number of bottles of single malt they'd consumed…

There was a good reason why Finn had hit the bottle, Luke conceded. His brother had died in front of him. He'd been wounded himself. There was trauma, deep and never spoken of.

He didn't want to get involved.

Too late. He already was.

'So why are you worried?' he growled, and started walking again, but Evie took his arm and made him stop. Here in the carpeted corridor of the private suites they could have some privacy.

'He dropped his clipboard.'

*He dropped his clipboard.* He let her words sink in. There wasn't a lot of basis there for worry.

But this was Evie, talking about Finn. Evie didn't do worry lightly.

Evie and Finn sparked off each other. Evie gave as good as she got. They'd make a good pair, Luke thought, but, wow, there'd be some fights.

Maybe that's what Finn needed. Fights. Someone to stand up to him.

His thoughts were flying tangentially. He was thinking about Finn. He was thinking about Tom.

He was thinking about Lily.

He didn't do personal concern. Or he hadn't. Suddenly he was surrounded on all sides.

In half an hour he had to take Lily home. Put her back into his bed. Make her something to eat…

Keep her safe.

No. Focus on Finn. Of the three worries, this was the easiest.

'Tell me what you're worried about.'

Evie exhaled and he thought this seemed liked a major decision, to talk to him about it.

'Wednesday night…he was walking down the corridor in front of me, carrying patient notes in one hand and a clipboard in the other. Heavy pile in the left. Clipboard in the right. He dropped the clipboard. I… We've been a bit tense with each other so I stood back; hoping he wouldn't turn around and see me. He stared down at the clipboard and then he stared at his hand. Swore. He set the notes down, put the clipboard on top of the notes and lifted them all in his left arm. Then he kept going, everything in his left arm, his right arm sort of tucked against him. And, Luke…yesterday in Emergency we had a guy who needed urgent stitching and I was flat out. Finn was passing. You know how he's always passing. I called for help and he stitched for me. It was tricky. This was a guy's face but Finn's good. Anyway, fifteen minutes later I finished what I was doing, went to the cubicle where Finn was working and he handed back over to me. "This is your job," he snapped. Okay, that's his usual style. But, Luke, I'd swear his right hand was trembling.'

Silence.

Luke stared out of the window and watched the Manly ferry chug slowly across the harbour.

His boss. A shaking hand.

It was probably nothing—only Evie didn't worry for nothing.

No matter how convoluted the gossip network of the Harbour became, Luke stayed detached. He liked to think he'd taught himself not to care, only of course he did care. From a distance.

Finn was a bad-tempered, surly, uncommunicative surgeon. He was one of the best surgeons Luke had ever worked with.

He was, like it or not, his friend.

How much of the single malt was he putting away?

So what to do? Head to Finn's office and say, 'I hear your hand's shaking?'

There was not one snowball's chance in a bush-fire of that happening, and of getting back out of the door if he did.

Besides, he needed to check on Tom. And then take Lily home.

Lily, of the gaunt face. Lily, who was too thin even before the gastro.

She'd needed this weekend to recover and it had ended like this.

'That's all I wanted to say,' Evie said, brisk again. 'I just thought...someone else should know.'

Gee, thanks, Luke thought morosely. Hand over your worries to me, why don't you?

But that wasn't fair, and he stopped himself from saying it. Evie could have taken her concerns straight to the medical director. Eric would then be bound to take them further. The legal implications of an impaired director of surgery would make Eric act whether he wished to or not.

Evie had chosen the kinder path.

'Thank you,' he said heavily.

'I'm sure you mean that,' she said dryly. 'Sorry, but I had to tell someone. Short of counting the whisky bottles in his garbage and confronting him with it, I didn't know what else to do. So can you fix Finn as well as Lily and her mother? I'll see to Uncle Tom.'

'That's hardly a fair division of labour.'

'No, but otherwise you're landed with everyone,' she said softly, and then she smiled. 'Because you care. I thought you'd escaped it but it seems even the great Luke Williams has to succumb to caring eventually.'

Lily wouldn't leave the hospital without seeing Tom. Luke had just come from Intensive Care but he detoured back again with her, carrying Lily's overnight bag, feeling strange. Feeling like a relative rather than a doctor.

As they walked through the corridors staff were watching, and as they neared ICU Lily took his hand.

The sensation was unnerving to say the least.

Once upon a time he and Hannah had had a relationship within this hospital. She'd held his hand whenever she could. Or rather her action had been… proprietary. From the time they'd started dating she'd announced their relationship in no uncertain terms.

Like Lily was doing now. Not like Hannah, who'd deliberately kissed him where colleagues would see, touched him whenever she could, called him sweet-heart in the wards, but, still, she was holding his hand and that was possessive enough.

Maybe she needed it for support. He glanced down at their linked fingers and her hold tightened.

'Don't,' she said.

'Don't what?'

'Look at our hands. Act as if it's normal. Isn't this what you want? For the staff to think we're a long-term couple? If we are, then holding hands is something we'd do all the time.'

It was.

It was also hard to get his head back to where it had been two days ago, to the idea that this was a pretend relationship so he could go on as he wanted to: independently.

'You think we should kiss, to make a bigger impression?' he said, thinking of Hannah.

'Long-term couples wouldn't,' she said. 'Kissing in corridors is tacky. Being caught in the on-call room was bad enough. Holding hands will do nicely, thank you.'

'We wouldn't want to seem tacky.'

'No, we wouldn't,' she said serenely. 'This couple has class.'

And then they were in ICU, and their hands could separate because all focus was on Tom. He still looked ashen, hooked up to every conceivable piece of technology the Harbour could throw at him, but amazingly he was smiling to see them.

'Here's trouble,' he whispered. 'I s'pose you're here to give me a lecture.'

'Not me,' Lily said roundly, and kissed him. 'I have more respect. Though I suspect Luke might be a bit angsty about his car.'

'His car?'

'He used it as a farm bike,' she said. 'I like it better now. It looks pre-loved.'

'That's me,' Tom whispered. 'If pre-loved looked battered.' He hesitated. 'Doc says I'll keep the leg, thanks to you guys.'

'I know you have two,' Lily said, still smiling. 'Trying to cut one off might seem a saving on socks, but think of all those left-foot shoes you'd have had to ditch.'

And Tom actually managed a grin. He was enchanted, Luke thought.

He wasn't the only one.

'I'm taking Lily home now,' he said, maybe more roughly than he intended. 'She's had a bit of a shock, too. She needs to rest.'

'Back to the farm?' Tom demanded.

'To my apartment.'

'Who's going to look after the farm?' No matter

how battered he was, Tom's focus would be on his horses.

'I'll drive up tomorrow,' Luke said. 'I'll sort something with the neighbours.'

'I'll come with you,' Tom said, and grimaced.

'No,' Luke said gently. 'Sorry, Tom, but with the damage you've done to your leg you'll need a while to get over it. You'll need a few days' physiotherapy.'

At least. Maybe a few weeks. It'd take time to get full function back.

'A few days...' Tom sounded appalled. He tried to sit up but Lily pressed him back on his pillows.

'Don't think about worst-case scenarios,' she said. 'For now you need to sleep. When the anaesthetic wears off properly, you'll be able to assess the damage for yourself.'

So stop worrying now, was her silent message, and she sent a warning glance to Luke.

She was right. What was he doing, talking long term when Tom was still in a post-operative haze? When things could still go wrong.

'But the farm...' Tom whispered.

'I'll go up every day,' Lily said, and Luke blinked. What?

'One of the mares is about to foal,' Tom whispered. 'Larkspur. And your little'un's too young to be left.'

'Merrylegs,' Lily said, smiling again. 'You reckon I'd let him fend for himself?'

'I know you wouldn't,' Tom said, and reached out and gripped her hand. 'You're a good kid. I dunno where Luke found you but I'm glad he did.'

'Me, too,' Lily said in a voice that was suddenly unsteady. 'And I bet he is, too, so that's three out of three. Aren't we all lucky?'

They didn't speak then until they were home. Home at Kirribilli Views, a two-minute drive from the hospital; home that wasn't a farm forty minutes' drive away.

There didn't seem much to say—or rather there was a lot to say and neither felt sure where to begin. Lily certainly didn't. She stood by Luke's side in the elevator. Luke was still carrying her bag and she thought, I've just taken over his life.

He rescued me from bedbugs and here I am, his live-in lover. About to lecture him about the care of his uncle.

It shouldn't be her business, whether he cared for his uncle or not, but it was. She'd lain still for an hour saving Tom's life and she was darned if she'd let him risk it again. She'd say something.

Soon.

The silence was getting oppressive.

And then the elevator door opened and Ginnie was in front of them and there was no such thing as silence.

'There you are!' It was a cry of triumph. 'I've been down and knocked three times already. I told John to let me know the minute you were discharged, Lily, because I wanted to catch you before Luke put you to bed.' She peeped a smile at them, and Lily groaned inside. 'As soon as I heard about the accident I dashed down to Pete's. His chef does the best beef and Burgundy pie. I've bought one for you because I expect you still won't want to come to Teo's party tonight. John tells me you were awesome,' she told Lily. 'You saved Luke's uncle. And he says the chopper guys say your farm's awesome as well,' she told Luke. 'I was thinking… I mean…not yet, obviously, while your uncle's unwell, but as soon as he's back on his feet John and I could drive up there. We could bring our own Sunday lunch. Do say yes. Now I'll just dash up and get the pie.'

'We don't need—' Luke started.

'Of course you do,' Ginnie retorted. 'Lily needs to try it. She needs to try everything. We can't believe you've hidden her for so long. Pete's Bar is right over the road from the hospital,' she explained to Lily. 'It's home away from home for half of the staff. Pete has half-price drinks on Wednesday, not that that's important. What is important is that John and I thought tomorrow night we'd take you both there for dinner. It's time you got to know us.'

That was said with a glare at Luke, like he'd somehow conspired to keep her hidden. Which, come to think of it, was just the impression he'd been after.

'Lily's still recovering from gastro,' Luke said, brusquely.

Lily thought, He hates this. Involvement.

Gossip?

Luke and Lily both.

'And as soon as I'm over it I'll be staying back at the farm,' Lily added. 'While Tom's recovering someone has to care for the horses.'

'What, alone?' Ginnie demanded. 'By yourself?'

'I'm an independent woman.'

'But John says it's only forty minutes from the hospital.' Ginnie was clearly struggling with information overload. 'The way Luke explained it, we thought it was hours away.'

'It's longer in peak traffic,' Luke said, but Ginnie wasn't listening.

'You could have come back for parties from there. I can't believe you'd live so close and not want to be part of the hospital scene. It has to stop. Lily, you don't like being isolated, surely?'

'It has advantages,' Lily told her.

'Like being allowed to go to bed when she needs to,' Luke said, and put his arm around her waist in a gesture that was almost rough. 'The pie's great, thank you, Ginnie, but I'll come up and collect it later, after Lily's settled.'

'You make me sound like a baby.' Lily tried to tug away but failed. 'We can both pop up and get the pie now.'

'No, we can't,' Luke said, sounding goaded. 'Bed.'

'Ooh,' said Ginnie.

'Ginnie...'

But Ginnie was grinning. 'I'm just going,' she said airily. 'I know when I'm not wanted. Tell you what, I'll pop the pie into the parcel box in the lobby. That way you can fetch it when you're fin...when you're ready.'

'Thank you,' Luke muttered, and turned Lily toward the door.

'Think nothing of it,' Ginnie said as Lily choked on sudden laughter. Ginnie backed into the elevator, Luke managed to get his key in the front door and propel her inside, he slammed the door behind them...

Lily couldn't help herself. The bubble of laughter wouldn't stay down one second longer.

Luke leaned on the door and glared at her, but it was so...it was so...

'It's not funny,' Luke growled.

'It's just what you want,' she managed. 'It couldn't be more perfect.' She smiled and smiled. 'Now that Tom's going to be okay.'

'There is that,' he said, and the trace of a smile appeared behind his glower.

'And you well and truly have a lover.'

'I do, don't I?' he said.

Her laughter caught. She met his gaze. Something locked. Held.

Laughter died.

'Lily…'

'They know about your farm,' she said, suddenly uncertain. The way he was looking at her…

'They do.'

'And your Uncle Tom.'

'Yes.'

'Can you bear it?'

'If I must,' he said softly, and instead of leaning against the door he was suddenly holding her by her shoulders. His gaze hadn't wavered.

'It's a hard call,' she whispered.

'It is,' he said. 'A package deal. The farm, Uncle Tom, and you.'

'Luke…'

'Enough,' he said. 'Enough, my beautiful Lily. Even though no one's watching, even though this doesn't corroborate our story one iota, even though it doesn't matter at all…I believe I need to kiss you.'

'Really?' She sounded hopeful, she thought. She sounded like a silly teenager.

But this was Luke.

'Really,' he said and proceeded to do just that.

# CHAPTER NINE

HIS kiss was strong and sweet and wonderful.

It was just like that first morning. Just like…

No. It was just like nothing.

It was just like now.

To say she was blown away was an understatement. The day's events had left her disoriented, wobbly, like her legs didn't belong to her. Now it seemed her body didn't belong to her. She was dissolving into a haze of heat and aching desire.

What was it with this man?

Charlie hadn't made her feel like this. Not even close.

Luke.

His hands were holding her close, and she felt like she was melting into him. Her breasts were crushed against his chest, and he felt like iron. Strength mixed with tenderness, she thought, dazed. It was the sexiest of combinations.

Restraint and desire.

For he was simply kissing. His mouth was exploring hers, nothing more. He held her close, and he kissed as if he wanted nothing more than simply to have this connection—and she felt fire.

For fire it was. The heat between their lips was indescribable. She was fusing to him, melting into him, wanting him with every shred of her being.

She was on tiptoe, wanting to be closer, closer…

Her hands were holding his face, feeling the roughness of his five o'clock shadow, loving the strength of his bone structure, quite simply…

Loving Luke.

As plain and as simple as that.

This man was like no one she'd met before but he wasn't a stranger. Something in him resonated as nothing had ever done before. The other half of her whole?

As simple and as complicated as that.

She was falling in love.

It was crazy, crazy, crazy, but it was there. She was falling in love with this man.

Or she would if he kept kissing her and no way did she want him to stop. She didn't care if this kiss broke records. She was holding him as hard as he was holding her. What was the record? Two days? Three? She was willing to give it a shot.

But he wasn't. Of course he wasn't.

She wasn't sure how long it lasted but it was Luke

who finally broke the contact. He tugged back and she almost glared. Only she couldn't quite glare. Not at Luke. Not at this man who'd just kissed her.

He was looking kind of fuzzy.

Her whole world was looking kind of fuzzy, she conceded. She'd just been kissed by Luke Williams. This man was seriously…

*Hers.*

She'd been thinking sexy. She'd been thinking hot. But when the word framed in her head it didn't come out like that.

Definitely the word was *hers.* Her man. She met his gaze and her heart twisted and she felt like she knew him better than she'd known any other living person. She felt like she was looking deep inside him.

And she saw shock. Dismay?

'Hey, it was you who kissed me,' she managed, but there was no way she could stop a tremor in her voice wobbling through. 'There's no reason to look like that. I'm not about to eat you.'

'Look like what? I wasn't thinking—'

'Yes, you are. Like I'm about to jump you. I'm not. Though it was a very nice kiss.' The tremor was getting better. She was getting better. More in control.

Liar. She was so out of control she wasn't sure what week it was.

'It was a very nice kiss,' he said, and his smile returned. Keep it light. That's what his smile said. Fine by her.

It had to be fine by her.

'But maybe not all that wise,' she said.

'No.'

'Not if we're living together. Mind, no one outside these walls would know.'

'Everyone outside these walls already knows,' he said, and the wariness was still there. 'They think we've been an item for years.'

'Well, then,' she said.

Where to take this from here?

What to do in a one-bedroom apartment on a Saturday night when you were pretending to be lovers?

When your body said you weren't pretending?

'I might head back to the hospital and do a ward round,' Luke said.

'A ward round on a Saturday night.'

'My current registrar's a bit unsure.'

So am I, she thought, but she didn't say so.

'Fine,' she managed. 'And you'll go back and see Tom?'

'Of course.' Things were formal. Absurdly formal.

'Remember to pick up our pie for dinner on the way back. It's in the parcel post in the foyer.'

'Yes, dear,' he said, and his smile was definitely back.

'That's good, then,' she said. 'I'll just watch the telly. I might do a bit of knitting on the side. Then…I don't know…dust the mahogany?'

'We don't have any mahogany.'

'That's a shame. It's my splinter skill.'

'Like rollerblading and horse riding.'

'That's right.' She hesitated. 'But far less dangerous. No one's ever yanked me off mahogany dusting, so you needn't worry at all. Luke, do tell Tom I'll go out to the farm tomorrow. I can't bear to think he'll worry about the dogs and horses. I can easily commute.' You could, too, she thought, but she didn't say it.

'You're not going to the farm. I'll drive up tomorrow and and organise things with Patty. She has a couple of sons who'll feed the animals.'

'You think Tom will be content with a neighbour's sons feeding his horses?'

'He doesn't want us up there.'

'Of course he does.'

'He likes his independence,' Luke snapped.

And Lily thought, Whoa.

'So…he's like you,' she said.

'He learned his lessons the way I learned mine. We don't depend on people.'

'No,' she said softly. 'You don't. But you do care for people.'

'Of course I care.'

'So kissing me now…'

'Wasn't such a good idea. Call it the culmination of one heck of a day.'

'I'd call it a lot more,' she said frankly. 'I've never felt like you made me feel just then. All wobbly at the knees.'

'You were wobbly at the knees before.'

'I was,' she admitted. 'But, then, I met you four days ago. My knees have been wobbly ever since.'

'Not because of me.'

'No.'

'Lily…'

'I know—it was an aberration.' She sighed. 'You're right, we're grown-up people and you have your independence and I have my mother. So the intersection of two worlds is impossible—except that we're still pretending it's possible.' She cocked her head to one side and considered. 'Luke, the way I'm feeling…'

'Wobbly kneed?'

'Yes,' she admitted. 'And it's not just gastro and Tom that's made them wobble. There's something about the way you make me feel… I know it's dumb but I can't help it and four weeks staying here… I think the sensible thing is for me to stay at the farm. Tom may well need four weeks of rehabilitation. I'm used to commuting a lot further than Tarrawalla. I can stay there happily until it's time to go back to Lighhouse Cove.'

'You can't go back to Lighthouse Cove.'

'I don't have a choice.' Her flash of being in control faded and she backed until she was leaning on the settee. She really was feeling wobbly.

'It's time you walked away from your mother.'

'And here's me thinking it's time you walked towards your Uncle Tom.'

'He doesn't need me.'

'He does. He just doesn't admit it.'

'And your mother admits it all the time.'

'At least I know where I stand.'

'Tied by the apron strings.'

'Don't,' she said wearily. 'I know she's difficult, but I've tried walking away in the past and I feel worse than if I stay. I loved my dad…'

'This is not your dad.'

'No, but—'

'It's past history. A promise made when you were twelve.'

'As your wife's death is past history,' she said softly. 'And the panic about losing people. It's not as easy as it sounds; ignoring history.'

'No.'

'So I can go to the farm.'

'You can go to bed.'

'Luke—'

'Enough,' he said roughly. 'Rest and then pie and leave any other decisions until morning. I'll fetch the pie on the way back. And no opening the door to visitors. I've had enough nosy-parkers in my life this weekend.'

'Am I included in that?'

'No,' he said roughly. 'Or at least…I'm not sure where you're included and I'm not sure I want to find out.'

He went back to the wards. Contrary to what he'd told Lily, his registrar was excellent. Evening visiting hours were in full swing. No patients wanted or needed to see him.

He ended up in Intensive Care. Tom was looking more stable by the moment but was fast asleep. Judy popped in; they discussed muscle and nerve damage, the need for rehab, and Judy's pride at how little residual damage she expected.

It was such a far call from where they'd been at midday, Luke felt dizzy.

'With the drugs I've given him, I doubt he'll surface until tomorrow,' Judy said. 'You needn't stand by his bed worrying he'll wake in pain. I promise it won't happen. You need to get back to Lily.'

'I…'

'She's a great girl,' Judy said softly. 'The whole hospital's happy for you.'

'Thank you.' He couldn't think what else to say.

'Will you stay at the farm and commute while Tom's in here? I gather that's where Lily's been hiding. Is her mother such a horror?'

Whoa… Evie. Surely she hadn't…

'This hospital has ears,' she said, grinning at the expression on his face. 'I was up seeing Hank Oliver in Six South, just about to walk out of his door, when I heard you and Evie talking.' She hesitated. 'What you said about Finn, too. It's not only Evie who's worried.'

'Nerve damage through drinking?'

'Unlikely,' she said. 'But possible. He'd never let me near to check.'

'Me neither.'

'Yeah, well, good luck with that one,' she said. 'Do your best. He might be an ill-tempered grouch but he's our ill-tempered grouch, and he's a fine surgeon. So…off to pack for the farm?'

'No.'

'Because of Lily's mother?'

'No!'

'Okay, none of my business,' Judy said, raising her hands in surrender. 'It doesn't help, though. You know as well as I do that keeping things to yourself in this hospital is impossible. Seemingly you've kept Lily to yourself for years but now you have every nose in this hospital twitching and they won't stop twitching until All Is Revealed.' She grinned and picked up her notes. 'Good luck and goodnight and welcome to the world of exposure. You know, it doesn't actually hurt. Sometimes it's even a power for good.'

He went back to the apartment. To Lily. They ate pie. They watched the grand finale of *Eurovision* on TV, one amazing, Lycra-clad act after another. Lily giggled.

He listened to Lily giggle and felt...like he needed not to feel.

Lily went to bed and closed the door behind her. He slept—badly—on the settee.

In the morning he woke at dawn, wrote Lily a note and left for the farm. He'd do what needed to be done and be back by lunchtime. Then he'd check on Tom, and spend the afternoon in his office catching up on medico-legal work. His day was thus mapped out, without Lily.

He reached the farm as the early morning sun

was still glistening through the trees. The leaves were wet with dew. The mountains were majestic in the background, the creek was rippling across the stones, the kookaburras were greeting the day and he felt the familiar tug of love he always had whenever he reached this place.

So why didn't he commute?

His uncle didn't want him to.

Or he didn't want to?

He thought back to the first lot of school holidays he'd spent at the farm, ten years old, and desperately lonely. It had been his first term break.

'It's too short a time to come home,' his mother had told him. 'Maybe you can come back here in summer.'

*Maybe.* The word had left him feeling sick.

He'd been the only kid left in the boarding house. The boarding master had been kind, but even Luke had been able to see he hadn't wanted him there. Finally, with a bravery that he still didn't believe he'd possessed, he'd rung an uncle he'd only heard of in conversation. 'I don't want to stay here...' He'd struggled not to cry but he hadn't succeeded.

'Your father doesn't want me messing in what's not my business,' his uncle had snapped, and hung up, but the next day his battered truck had pulled up outside the boarding house.

'The kid'll be better at my place,' he'd told the boarding master, and had broken every rule in the book by simply loading Luke into the cab of the truck and leaving without parental permission.

Back at the farm Tom had barely spoken. He'd shown Luke a bedroom and told him he was expected to look after himself.

The next day he'd given him a colt and shown him how to train him. Checkers. Luke's life had looked up from that moment.

But rough kindness apart, they'd lived separate lives. Tom had barely spoken to him, but at the end of each term—and finally most weekends—the truck would turn up at school and Luke would find himself back at the farm. The deal was Luke didn't get in Tom's way and Tom didn't get in his. When Luke had been able to afford it he'd bought the place next door, which Tom seemed to approve of, even if he only signified it by a grunt.

Today's outburst by Tom, his approval of Lily, his story of an old love affair…that had been the most he'd heard from Tom, ever.

He'd held Tom up as an example. How to live without needing people.

Maybe it was an illusion.

Was it okay to admit to needing people? Needing Lily?

No. He didn't need Lily, he knew that.

But maybe Lily needed him.

He could keep her safe.

Right. Like he'd kept Hannah safe.

Lily on Glenfiddich… The fear…

He wasn't making sense, even to himself. He raked his hair and wondered what he was doing staring at mountains when there was work to be done. He needed to head over to Tom's and feed the dogs. He need to check the cattle, put out the hay, check the horses.

And tomorrow?

Lily had offered to come up here. She was working nights. She could be here in the daytime, he could be here at night. Every night.

But…it seemed dangerous, just as it had when he'd first bought this place and wondered whether he could commute.

'Every night,' Tom had said, startled. 'What would you want to do that for? Your work's your life, boy. Don't you forget it.'

He'd forgotten it for a bit, and his work had killed Hannah.

His head felt like it was going round in circles. To let Lily come up here, day after day, to be here by herself…

It wasn't going to happen. He'd speak to Patty, employ one of her sons, get on with his life.

He headed off to feed the cattle, knowing he had a fight on his hands. He'd known Lily for, what, four days, and already he knew she wouldn't take this lying down.

She had to accept it. This was none of her business. The plan was she was to stay in his apartment for four weeks. Period.

He needed to stay in control. He needed to keep Tom's wishes in mind. He needed to maintain independence for both of them.

Despite Lily.

Plans didn't always come off, especially when three people were making them and Luke was only one of three. On Tuesday morning Lily finished work, took her suitcase from Luke's apartment and headed for the farm. Luke had no say. She'd organised it directly with Tom.

'I know you don't want me on your place,' she told Luke. 'So I won't be on your place. You've organised Patty's son to feed the animals. He can keep on looking after your place but Tom's asked me to look after his. I'm sleeping at his house. This is an arrangement between me and Tom so, as you're very keen on saying, butt out, it's none of your business.'

'You can't commute.' She was looking better but she was still pale. Still too thin. A weekend of bullying her to eat could only achieve so much.

'Yes, I can,' she said. 'You could too if you wanted, but you needn't worry. All the hospital knows why I'm doing what I'm doing, and they all think our love affair's still going strong. Knowing I'm helping Tom just adds to their belief that ours is a truly authentic love affair. With you working days and me working nights, and me living at the farm and you here, we can have a love affair without ever seeing each other. That's just the way you like it.'

Just the way he liked it. It wasn't. Neither did he like it that he saw Lily only in passing, as she arrived or left for work, or when he chanced on her in Tom's ward. It wasn't enough.

Tom was recovering well, accepting the need for rehabilitation, knowing he wouldn't be back at the farm for weeks. He was tickled pink that Lily was staying in his house.

Lily was making him talk. A week after the accident Luke walked in on Tom in the rehabilitation ward and Tom was chuckling.

Tom didn't chuckle. He was a recluse. A loner. But there was something about Lily…

'You didn't go up to the farm for the weekend,' Tom said accusingly.

'I was on call.'

It was Monday morning. Lily must be about to go off duty. She was wearing her agency uniform. She looked neat and prim and cute.

The farm must be doing her good, he thought. She looked much more relaxed than she had last week. She'd gained a bit of colour. Maybe she'd been riding one of Tom's horses.

Not Glenfiddich. The thought of her on his half-wild colt when she was on her own on the farm was unthinkable. He'd made her promise not to go near.

'You needn't worry,' she'd said. 'I get the boundary thing. Over your boundary I will not step.'

But Tom had horses, too. Was she riding them with no one around?

He wanted to ask.

He knew she'd react with anger.

He stood in the doorway and thought about retreating.

'Hey,' Tom said. 'Luke. You want to see me walk?'

There was no retreating from a statement like that. He watched as his uncle proudly manoeuvred the walking frame to the door, then let it go, held the rail along the corridor and made it all the way along to the nurses' station.

He and Lily stood side by side, like two proud parents. Lily clapped him on.

As Tom reached the end, he glanced down and Lily was smiling and sniffing back tears.

She'd only known Tom for a week. She was that involved?

'Isn't it wonderful?' she whispered.

And he thought, Yes, it is. And, yes, she was. But to wear her heart on her sleeve…didn't she understand about being hurt?

Didn't she understand how much love hurt?

'Tom's enjoying this,' she said softly, as Tom inched his way back to them. 'Despite his leg. He's making friends. Are you sure he really wants to be a loner?'

'He's made a good fist of it if he doesn't.'

'Maybe he's just good at disguising need,' she told him, and went back to encouraging Tom.

Tom was trying so hard, Luke thought, and then he thought I'd try hard, too, if Lily was expecting it of me.

'I have tomorrow off,' Lily was telling Tom. 'If the physio okays it, would you like me to take you to Coogee? Do you know it? I've only just discovered it; it's the most gorgeous little beach only twenty minutes from here. We could do your exercises in the ocean baths. Fun!'

Fun? This was Tom she was talking to, Luke thought. Tom didn't do fun.

But Tom was looking at Lily with delight. 'Ocean baths?'

'Rock pools,' she said. 'They're fabulous. What if I pick you up at ten?'

'You'll need help getting into the water,' Luke said, and then, before he knew it, he found himself offering. 'I'll come with you.'

'I don't want you bothering with me,' Tom growled—but he hadn't said that to Lily.

'It's okay. I can arrange time off.'

'There's no need,' Lily told him. 'Tom and I will manage. Meanwhile, I'm off to the farm to sleep.' She kissed Tom, an extraordinary gesture to Tom, who treated invasion of privacy with horror. 'I haven't slept so well in years as on your farm. It'll be hard when I have to leave.'

'Maybe you could stay,' Tom said, to Luke's further shock. 'I mean…you need somewhere to board, right?'

'I'll be returning to Lighthouse Cove,' Lily said, sounding regretful. 'But it's a lovely offer. Thank you.'

She left—and Tom watched her go with regret.

'Do something,' he snapped. 'She's gold. You'd seriously let her go back to this Lighthouse Cove she talks about?'

'I don't have a choice,' Luke said. 'It's her business.'

'Bunkum. It's our business. I made a fool of myself once, and you messed around with that selfish woman you married. But this time… If I was forty years younger…' He shoved himself from the corridor railing and lurched toward his walking frame, only just managing to grab it. 'Leave me be,' he growled as Luke moved to help. 'Go after your woman if you want something to do. Her business? A man'd be mad to think that.'

# CHAPTER TEN

AT TEN on Tuesday Lily arrived at the Harbour to take Tom to the beach.

She was growing really fond of Tom.

So much for anonymity, she thought ruefully as she passed through the hospital on the way to Tom's ward. She'd come to Sydney aching to be a nobody and here she was, involved up to her neck. She was part of the Harbour team. She was Tom's friend. She was Luke's pretend lover.

But her involvement was an illusion, she thought as she was greeted by staff members all through the hospital. It was a part of the deception that was her relationship with Luke, but at the same time it was a taste of something she'd never known.

Until now, gossip had seemed vicious and hurtful. Here it was a way of life. A part of belonging. The Harbour was closing round her, enfolding her as one of its own, and the sensation was extraordinary.

At Lighthouse Cove she'd been the daughter of a man who'd died owing money to half the town and of a woman whose morals were questionable. She'd been shunned as a 'bad lot' all through her teen years. During her training in Adelaide, at the end of every shift she'd faced the long drive back to Lighthouse Cove. She hadn't had time to join in social fun. She was considered an outsider. She was used to being an outsider. When she'd come here what she'd wanted was to be anonymous, but now…

She was a member of the Harbour team.

Tom's friend.

Luke's lover.

The concept of belonging was an illusion, she told herself savagely. It had to end but it was messing with her head. It was like a siren song, dragging her in.

Luke had it for real, she thought, but he didn't want it. He didn't know how lucky he was. She had to go back to Lighthouse Cove. She had to leave Luke and everyone around him.

She walked into Tom's ward—and Luke was there.

Both men were casually dressed. Tom was already settled into a wheelchair. Luke had a bag full of beach-towels slung over his shoulder. They looked relaxed and happy and ready to go.

They took her breath away.

*Luke took her breath away.*

'You're two minutes late, Nurse,' Luke said, mockingly severe. 'Tom and I have been waiting and waiting.'

He was wearing jeans. His short-sleeved, open-necked shirt displayed a hint of the muscles of his chest. His hair looked ruffled.

His hair always looked ruffled, Lily thought. He had the most gorgeous hair. He had the most gorgeous smile…

'I've borrowed John's SUV,' he said, while her thoughts flew everywhere. 'I figured it'd be easier to get the wheelchair in and out.'

'You're coming with us?'

'I said I would.'

'But I didn't think…' She drew in breath. 'I mean…don't you have surgery?'

'I have an excellent registrar and an easy list,' he said. 'I need to be back by three for a cleft lip and palate but Tom will be ready for a sleep by then.'

'I won't,' Tom said indignantly. 'But if you need to be back by three, why are we hanging round here? Push.'

Luke chuckled and pushed.

Lily followed, feeling flummoxed.

She hadn't intended this. She thought, It's dangerous. But then Luke was the one who worried about dangerous.

They passed Reception on the way out and Evie was there.

'It's the Williams family.' Evie smiled. 'Have a lovely day.'

'Thank you,' Lily said, and glanced at Tom and then at Luke and saw similar expressions on both their faces.

*The Williams family...*

It didn't exist. Another illusion.

Dangerous.

The beach was gorgeous. The day was gorgeous.

They wheeled Tom down the ramp, helped him into the water. Tom's legs were white from years on the farm where long protective pants were the norm. The scar on his thigh stood out stark and dreadful. Luke expected him to sit in the shallows and do his exercises.

Instead he swam. Luke hadn't even known he could swim. Lily swam too, and he watched.

He watched as they swam, then he watched as Lily helped his uncle go through his exercises, then he watched as they duck-dived for stones.

'I'm playing lifesaver,' he told them when Tom accused him of laziness, but he wasn't.

He was watching Tom come out of his shell. And he was watching Lily. In her simple, green, one-piece bathing suit, with her wet curls spiralling down her back, with her eyes sparkling…

She was entrancing.

He was watching his uncle fall under her spell.

He was falling under her spell himself.

He should join in, but if he duck-dived he'd brush against her body. He wanted it—but he wasn't going there.

Need. Desire. Things he'd put away for a lifetime were suddenly front and foremost.

'What is it?' she demanded as she surfaced and saw him watching. 'You're watching me as if I have two heads.'

'One head's enough.'

'So's one and a half legs,' she retorted, after a thoughtful stare back at him. 'That's all Tom has and he's beating me at duck-diving every time. You don't want to compete?'

'No.'

'More fool you,' Tom said, and chuckled, tossed the next stone and dived.

He abandoned lifesaving. He went and swam in the bay, hard and fast and long.

Alone.

They swam until they were exhausted. They ate fish and chips on the foreshore and Tom started drooping. Lily brushed the sand from her toes and slipped on her flip-flops, decreeing time out was over.

'Back to the Harbour,' she said. 'Tom, you need a sleep, and you, Dr Williams, have surgery scheduled.'

'Luke!'

'Luke,' she said, and smiled.

Oh, that smile…

'Are you going back to the farm tonight?' he managed.

'Of course.'

'Let me take you to dinner here instead.' Where had that come from?

He knew where it had come from. From need, pure and simple.

'She has to feed the horses,' Tom said.

'Okay, then,' Luke said, driven against the ropes. 'We'll have dinner at the farm. I'll stay the night and come back early tomorrow.'

She surveyed him with caution, as if he'd just proffered a peace offering and it might just explode. 'But you don't like commuting,' she said at last.

'I'll make an exception.'

'That's big of you.'

He ignored the sarcasm. 'I'll bring up a couple of Pete's pies.'

'They are good,' she said, weakening. 'Okay.'

She'd accepted.

Dinner. On the farm. With Lily.

He thought of the restaurant meals Hannah used to love. Dinner in any restaurant within a mile of this hospital meant every mouthful, every nuance was reported back to the gossip machine. Hannah had thrived on gossip.

Lily was different. He could see dinner on the farm with Pete's pies was a temptation where dinner anywhere else wasn't.

'We'll stay in separate houses,' Lily said, cautiously.

'A man'd be a fool...' Tom retorted, and Lily grinned.

'You stay out of this. Isn't the older generation supposed to keep up moral standards?'

'What fun is there in moral standards?' Tom demanded. 'And the whole hospital thinks you're sleeping together anyway.'

So even the patients thought it. Luke rolled his eyes—and caught Lily doing exactly the same.

He laughed and Lily laughed and things suddenly lightened.

Filled with hope?

'Okay,' Lily said. 'If you bring pies, I'll supply wine. Tom's veranda at eight?'

'We have a date,' he said gravely.

'Excellent,' she said. 'Pete's pies are awesome.'

And that was that.

He watched Lily feed the last of the chips to flying seagulls, going to enormous effort to make sure a one-legged bird was well fed.

That was Lily, he thought.

Hope?

Suddenly he had it in spades.

'Exactly how long have you known this woman?'

It was Finn—of course.The man was always where he was least expected to be.

Luke had less than an hour to get to the farm. He'd just repaired a cleft lip and palate, the procedure had taken longer than expected and even for his boss, he wasn't interested in stopping.

'I can't remember,' he lied. 'I need to get on.'

'The way you look at her…you're thinking of making it legal?'

'What, marriage?' That was enough to make him pause.

'That's what the grapevine's saying. The girls in Accounts are taking bets on you having another society bash. Will your parents come over again?'

In your dreams, he thought. A wedding like the last one…

Hannah's parents had serious money. His parents

had come from Singapore. He still woke in a cold sweat thinking of that wedding.

'If anyone's to be married it should be you,' he told Finn. 'I've done my time. You haven't even stuck your toe in the water.'

'You can have a lot more fun without marriage.'

'I don't see you having fun.' He surveyed his friend with concern and decided to be blunt. 'It seems to me you're using women to distract yourself from something else. Pain?'

'Leave it.'

'So…you can talk to me about Lily and marriage and I can't talk to you about the pain in your right arm?'

'Who said anything about pain?'

He wasn't landing Evie in it. 'This is the Harbour,' he said mildly. 'Knowledge permeates its walls and then oozes out again.'

'The walls have it wrong.'

'The walls don't think so. What exactly hurts?'

'I've strained a muscle,' Finn snapped. 'It's getting better.'

'So who's seen it?'

'No one needs to see it. It's healing.'

'Can I take a look?'

'No.'

'Finn…'

'Get out of here. Go find your woman,' Finn snapped. 'They help.'

Luke hesitated. *They help.* The statement hung. That's what he'd thought, that Finn was using women to blot something out.

Physical pain or mental?

'Maybe you need to talk to a shrink,' he said softly. 'Hell, Finn, what you've been through… Let me make you an appointment.'

Uh-oh. He'd got that wrong. Finn's face tightened with anger. If looks could kill, Luke would be dead right now.

But Finn was his friend and he wasn't backing down. 'You know you need help,' Luke said. 'Why can't you admit it?'

'You know where you can put your help.' Finn stalked to the door, lifted his right arm—which didn't shake—and swept it hard across the bench.

Patient notes went flying, and Finn was gone. The door slammed so hard behind him it almost came off its hinges.

That went well, Luke thought. *Or not.*

He stared at the closed door. He thought about going after him. Thought it'd be useless.

Besides, he was having dinner with Lily.

* * *

He collected the pies—beef and burgundy, and chicken and leek. They smelled fantastic. Pete wrapped them in cloth with directions about reheating. 'Put 'em in a microwave and I'll come after you with a cleaver. Treat 'em right. You'll never win a lady with a soggy pie.'

'Who said anything about winning a lady?' he demanded. But Pete had already moved on to his next Harbour client, his next piece of gossip.

About twenty pairs of eyes followed him out the door of the pub. Counting pies.

Tomorrow they'd know he hadn't come back to Kirribilli tonight, he thought, and then he thought, So what?

One way to stop gossip—pretend to be in love.

A better way to stop gossip… Acknowledge you were.

He stopped short, feeling…discombobulated.

*In love.*

He drove all the way to Tarrawalla and the two words stayed with him all the way.

Lily was waiting. She had the table set on Pete's veranda.

He wasn't to be invited inside?

She took the pies and sniffed her appreciation.

'I'll put them in the Aga to reheat,' she said and he blinked.

'You're using the Aga?' As far as he knew, the slow combustion fire stove hadn't been used in his lifetime.

'Why wouldn't I? It's fabulous.' She slipped inside and returned with wine.

She was wearing jeans and an oversized wind-cheater. She had mosquito coils burning by the table.

Romantic dinner by candlelight?

Dinner by mosquito coils.

'How did the cleft palate repair go?' she asked, and that took him back all over again. He hadn't told her what he'd been doing.

But, then, those Harbour walls…

'He'll be okay. We'd been hoping to wait until he was a little older but his local hospital rang this morning. He was starting to suffer respiratory distress so we had to bring it forward. His mum's been beside herself but it's gone well; she can sleep easy tonight.'

'That's great,' she said simply. 'Those pies will take fifteen minutes to reheat. You want to take a walk, or just sit and listen to the frogs?'

'Frogs are great.'

'Aren't they?' she said, and shut up and listened.

She wasn't expecting him to talk, he thought. She wasn't expecting him to do anything.

Nothing.

He'd spent four hours this afternoon in nerve-racking surgery. He'd made the best possible job he could of tiny Joshua McFaddon's disfigured mouth. He was delighted with the result, but it had taken it out of him. He'd been up since five.

He was physically exhausted and Lily was simply saying listen to frogs.

The silence deepened, and the thought that had been playing in his head all the way up here grew louder. And louder.

'I believe I'd like to try living with you,' he said, before he even knew what he intended to say.

The words hung.

*I believe I'd like to try living with you.*

Where had that come from? The desire.

It had just happened. He wanted to live with Lily. Simple as that.

He didn't want the huge emotional roller-coaster of courtship, engagement, wedding. Not the romantic fantasy. But this need was growing more powerful by the moment. To have this restful woman beside him.

But she was looking...flabbergasted.

'Live,' she said, floundering. 'You mean...like

housemates? Your bedroom at one end of the house, mine at the other?'

'No,' he said. For she might be restful but she was also beautiful. And sexy. And so desirable she made a man burn. 'I believe I mean live together as in what the Harbour believes we're doing right now.'

'For three weeks?'

'I suspect I'd like to make it permanent. It feels like it would be great—being permanent.'

She was looking at him like he was nuts. Maybe he was. He shouldn't decide he wanted a permanent relationship when he'd known her for less than a week, he thought, but it felt like he'd known her for much longer. She seemed…the part of him that was missing.

If she was, she wasn't about to join up again. 'You've lost your mind,' she said.

'I'm just saying what I'm feeling,' he told her, trying to figure it out as he went. 'I've never met anyone like you. When I'm with you I feel like I've come home.'

She tried to smile. 'That's because I smell of the hay I've been hauling.'

'There is that,' he conceded.

'So you agree it's nonsense.'

And suddenly he thought, I've scared her.

'Lily, I'm not pushing for anything you don't want,'

he said hastily. 'I'm simply saying what I feel. With Hannah…we were an item for two years before I proposed. We were engaged for another year while she organised the wedding of the millennium. For all that time I didn't feel like I'm feeling now. Like this is where I should be.'

'On the veranda of your uncle's farm?'

'With you,' he said softly. 'If you'll agree, I'd love you to come back to my apartment,' he said, urgently now. 'Lily, we decided to be pretend lovers. Let's see if we can be real ones.'

'Lovers.' She still thought he had a kangaroo loose in the top paddock, he thought. This woman was a highly trained medic. Any minute now she'd produce a strait-jacket to stop him hurting himself.

'I know it's fast…'

'Yeah, I feel like I've missed something,' she said warily. 'The process that goes before. Like dates and stuff. We haven't actually slept together yet, have we? I mean, I haven't forgotten anything important?'

'I… No.'

'There you go.' She sounded like she'd decided to humour him. 'No matter what the Harbour thinks, one kiss does not a relationship make.' She took a deep breath, moving on. 'Luke, I'm hungry. Maybe that's your problem. Hunger makes people do weird things. Stay where you are. Don't move. I'll see if the Aga's done its magic.'

The Aga had. So had Pete. The pies were wonderful.

Lily ate hers with one eye on the pie and one eye on him. That was in case he suddenly developed strange twitches, he thought, or saw dancing elephants.

He found himself smiling as he ate. This really was ridiculous. He was out of his mind.

But he still felt exactly the same, like the woman across the table was part of him.

She wasn't eating enough. He wanted to bully her to eat more but he thought he had more important things he wanted her to agree to tonight.

'Walk?' he said when they'd eaten, and she was still watching him. He rose and held out his hand. 'Please.'

'I need to do the dishes.'

'Blighty,' he called. 'Patch.' As the dogs hared up the veranda steps he put dirty plates down and the washing up was done. Sort of.

'Sorted,' he said, and she choked.

'Of all the… Typical surgeon!'

'What?'

'No finesse. You were supposed to offer to wash, thus earning brownie points.'

'Would you consider living with me if I washed them?'

'You're ridiculous.'

For an answer he held out his hand again. 'Walk. Please.'

She hesitated, and then cautiously took a step forward.

Excellent. He took her hand and he led her down the veranda steps, down to the creek and into the night.

They walked silently, the dogs following at their heels. Silence was almost their usual state, he thought. That was fine by him; he'd been raised in silence and it was a friend.

His fingers were linked with Lily's. In a moment the silence would end, her fingers would withdraw and the moment would be gone, but in the silence was a promise of a future.

Hope.

They followed the creek along the bank, skirting trees, boulders, fallen timber. At one point they had to cross the creek to get further, stepping over widely spaced rocks. He wanted to help her but she was intent on coping herself.

She reached the other side and he took her hand again.

She didn't resist.

'I've fallen in love,' he said gently, at last, and the words hung in the night sky.

'That sounds…easy to do,' she said cautiously. 'People do it all the time. Only not with me.'

'A man'd be mad not to.'

'Because I helped your uncle?'

'Because you're wonderful.'

'Okay, I helped your uncle and I'm wonderful,' she said, and he could tell she was struggling to sound placid. 'Two compliments do not lovers make.'

'I know,' he said ruefully. 'It's too soon. But I'd love you to come back to my apartment, to see if we can make it work.'

She stopped then, turning in the moonlight so she could see his face. She looked troubled.

'That's another thing I don't understand. Why would you want to go back to your apartment when you could stay here?'

'Maybe we *could* stay here,' he said, thinking that with this woman anything was possible. Even a home was possible. 'But not while you're working nights. I don't like this. I'm away during the day. Tom's not here. What if something happens?'

'I'm not Hannah,' she said, and he flinched.

'I know that.' He raked his hair, knowing he needed to get a handle on what he was feeling.

Knowing it was too huge for any handle. 'But I'd never want a marriage where I couldn't reach you.'

'Who's talking marriage?' she demanded, astounded.

'Okay, I'm not,' he said hastily. 'Not yet. But even now, when we're little more than friends, I hate you being here by yourself.'

'We're *nothing* more than friends,' she said, calm and sure. 'And I love being here. I don't need you to know that I'm safe. I'm a big girl. I'm responsible for my own safety. I don't take risks—or not many. You know I won't ride Glenfiddich, even though I'd love to, but even if I did, I don't want anyone wrapping me in cotton wool. If that's the kind of relationship you want, then thank you very much but no.'

'I think,' he said carefully, 'that right now I'd be content with any relationship you'd be prepared to give.' He took her hand back in his and looked down at their linked fingers in the moonlight. She looked up at him, and he knew her answer was no.

'I have my mother,' she said, and it was like saying, 'Step away.'

He didn't. He held her more strongly still. 'I won't let your mother hurt you.'

'You'll protect me from my mother as well?'

'From anything that threatens you. The way I'm feeling…'

'Well, you can stop feeling,' she said, suddenly angry. She tugged back as if he'd suddenly shown signs of the plague.

'Lily…'

'I'm my own person,' she said. 'Or I'm trying to be. I'm struggling really hard to have a life. With Mum like she is, I only manage it in snatches, but in those snatches I'm not about to be cocooned.'

'I wouldn't—'

'Of course you would,' she said. 'That's why you don't commute from here, isn't it—because you think that if you live here then you and your Uncle Tom might learn to depend on each other. You both hold onto your precious independence because anything else is too scary. And me? You'd take me back to the Harbour, back to the Sydney Scandal Central, you'd ensconce me in your sterile apartment and you'd keep me safe. You'd bring me up here when you're free to watch me. I bet you'd even offer to buy me a nice quiet mare.'

That idea had crossed his mind. She met his gaze and saw.

'Ha!' She tried to smile but it didn't come off.

'Do you think,' he said cautiously, moving sideways, 'that apart from the safety thing, a relationship might be possible?'

'Do you mean do I find you sexy? Of course I do.'

He reached for her hand again but she stepped away fast.

'Of course you're sexy,' she said. 'You're so sexy you make my toes curl. And you're kind and clever and a brilliant doctor, and I love the way your hair does that really cute kick at the sides. And you have the best horses. But you won't let me ride them. You come with a past, and that past is problematic. And I come with a mother and she's more so.'

'I can fix—'

'Your past? I don't think so. How do you walk from the shades of a dead wife and child? Hannah will always be with you. I suspect you'll always want her to be.'

He thought about that, trying to be fair. In some ways, she was right.

Hannah had been a gorgeous, vibrant girl who'd pulled him from his studious, solitary life and introduced him to fun. It hadn't worked—he'd been too infatuated to see past her glossy exterior until it was too late—but he was grateful for what she'd given him. She'd died carrying his child.

She would always be a part of him.

'And I'll always be with my mother,' she said, softly, watching his face. 'Of the two, I'd choose Hannah. At least you can keep the parts of her you loved and let the rest go.'

'You can't do that with your mother?'

'No,' she said, and sighed. 'Enough. This was a lovely walk. It was a huge compliment, saying you'd like what's between us to go further, but I'm old and wise enough now to know what's possible and what's not.'

She took his hands back in hers and looked down at them, steadily, surely. She was bracing herself, he thought, and here it came.

'Luke, let's be honest,' she said. 'You wouldn't want to be tied in a relationship with me. You'd want to cocoon me and I'd kick against the traces and you'd hate it. My mother would be included and you'd hate it. The threat of what happened to Hannah would always hang over us and our lives would be impossible. Tonight we had great pie, some lovely wine, a gorgeous walk, but now it's over.'

And before he knew what she intended, she stood on tiptoe and kissed him, lightly, a feather touch, her lips brushing his so fleetingly it was as if he was imagining it. And when he went to hold her close she backed away.

'Your house is thataway,' she said, pointing through the trees where he could just see his veranda light. He'd left the car and walked to Tom's. 'Mine's in the opposite direction. The dogs will take me home. You need to go home by yourself. You

and Tom have lives apart. You only know two ex-
tremes—apart or so close you'd cage me. But with
my mother I'm already caged, and that cage is a long
way from your side.'

She didn't sleep. Of course she didn't. How could a
girl sleep after such a night?

She lay in the dark and thought about living with
Luke Williams. Sharing his bed. Sharing his life.

Impossible, impossible, impossible—but, oh, to
be asked...

For him to feel as she was feeling seemed a miracle. A miracle that couldn't be taken further.

Maybe she should try it, she thought in the small
hours. She could return to his apartment and see if
she could make it work.

But if she put one toe in the water her whole body
would follow. If she slept with him...

She knew she'd melt.

'I'm weak,' she whispered, and she knew she was.

'And I can't be,' she said. 'I'd break my heart. To
let myself love him and then have to walk away...'

Oh, but to let him walk away now...

She rolled over in bed and stared across the valley.
She could still see his veranda light in the distance.

Was he lying in bed thinking the same?

Thinking about sharing his life?

He wasn't talking about sharing. He was talking about tugging her into his life and holding her close. They were two different things and she was wise enough to see it.

Sleep wouldn't come. Her stomach was hurting. Avoid stress? Ha. She gave up, warmed a hot-water bottle to alleviate the cramps and headed out onto the veranda, where the dogs lay on an ancient couch. They roused and wagged their tails and shifted along, as if this was her place as well.

She lay, and the dogs sprawled on top.

'See, I'm hopeless at being alone,' she told them. 'Is it time I went home to my mother?'

He dropped by the next morning, just at dawn. She woke to find him staring down at her, woman under dogs.

To say she felt at a disadvantage was an understatement.

'Do you mind?' she managed. 'This is my bedroom.'

'So I see.' He sounded stunned.

He was looking gorgeous, she thought, in tailored pants and his crisp, white shirt. He wasn't wearing a tie but it'd be in his car, she decided, ready to be popped on at need.

She was in her ancient nightgown. She'd be smelling of mosquito repellent. The only thing she could put on at need was dog hair.

She wanted, quite desperately, to be in her nice, anonymous, nursing uniform. On level pegging. Right now she felt like a charity case. Someone to be looked after. That was how he thought of her, wasn't it?

'You've slept with the dogs,' he said.

'Mmm.' She tried to act casual. She yawned and stretched and the dogs yawned and stretched with her. 'We like it out here.'

'You sleep outside when you're here by yourself?' He sounded appalled.

'I have the dogs.'

'I'm commuting,' he said grimly. 'I'll stay at my farm until Tom comes home.'

'Until…'

'Okay, maybe I'll commute after he comes home as well,' he snapped. 'Maybe I need to. He's even more pig-headed than you.'

'That'd be hard.'

'I'll see you tonight,' he said, brusque again.

'I'll be going to bed early tonight. I'll thank you not to check on me.'

'Lily—'

'Independence,' she said.

'It's your mantra. You want it for yourself, so give it to me. Say byebye to Daddy, guys.'

She lifted two dog paws and waved them at Luke. Luke spun on his heel and left.

Discombobulated didn't begin to describe how she felt as he walked away.

# CHAPTER ELEVEN

THE next night Lily went back to the night shift. She put her head down and worked. She tried to put Luke out of her mind.

That was pretty hard when the entire hospital was treating them as a couple. 'Would you and Luke like to come out with us? What are you and Luke doing at the weekend? Can we come up and visit?'

She got pretty good at avoiding invitations, and she assumed Luke was doing the same. 'Sorry, we're a bit overwhelmed with work now that Tom's in hospital. Maybe when he's better…'

When Tom was better, she'd be gone.

But still there was this insidious sweetness. Belonging. She'd never felt it before and it was almost overwhelming her. If she really did belong here… If she really was in love with Luke…

No. Reality was very different. She'd aimed for anonymous; she had to keep reminding herself that anonymous was what she wanted.

\* \* \*

Luke was doing the same, knocking back invitations and trying to avoid being with Lily in a work capacity.

Professionally they hardly saw each other. Lily worked the night shift, Luke worked days. He made sure she wasn't rostered to Theatre— 'Personal relationships distract me when I'm working,' he told Elaine, and Elaine raised her brows but made sure his theatre roster didn't include Lily—and he didn't need to see her at all.

But he did need to check she was still okay. He dropped by Tom's farm every morning, making sure she was safe home before he left for work. She didn't seem to appreciate it but he did it all the same.

Twice there were late-night lacerations where he was called in and Lily needed to assist. She was kindness itself to the patients but she was business-like in her dealings with him.

'I can see why you can't have her in Theatre,' Elaine told him, thoughtful. 'When you see each other it's like you both put on masks. Mr and Mrs Rigid. I don't understand. The whole hospital knows you're an item—why not relax and enjoy it?'

And then, toward the end of the second week, she probed deeper. 'You two haven't had a fight, have you? It'd be such a shame if we finally found out about your love life only to have it end. Your Lily makes every patient feel like the sun's come out, but when you come into the room it's like a cloud descends. I'm sensing domestic disharmony.'

Everyone was probing. Nurses, Luke thought dourly. Once upon a time they'd known their place, but Elaine was ten years older than he was, she'd been at the Harbour for ever and the only doctor she treated with deference was Finn.

There was another problem. Finn.

He couldn't do anything about Finn, as he couldn't do anything about Lily. Nothing but worry.

And, of course, this was the Harbour. He wasn't the only one worrying.

'Is Lily eating okay?' Evie was probing, as seemingly the whole hospital was probing about Lily. 'She's still looking pale. She shrugged it off when I asked but, if I were you, I'd push for blood tests. We should have had them done when she fainted.'

'She's under stress,' he said shortly, knowing what Lily's reaction would be if he pushed any such thing.

'Because of her mother?'

'Yes. And she shouldn't be driving back and forth to the farm.' He raked his hair. 'But I can't stop her.'

'Why doesn't she shift from agency to permanent?' Evie suggested. 'The hospital would employ her in a minute. We could organise her onto the day shift and you could travel back and forth together.'

'She doesn't want permanent work.'

'Because?'

'Evie...'

'Okay.' She held up her hands in surrender. 'I know. Relationships are out of bounds. I should know that—I'm hopeless at them. I'll butt out. But she's pale, Luke. Fix it.'

She *was* pale, Luke thought.

She didn't want him interfering.

When Tom had been in hospital for two weeks—another week and he'd be ready for home—Luke dropped into his ward and found Lily perched on his bed. They were intent on Tom's exercises, and for a moment he could watch them both, unnoticed.

Tom was looking great.

He tried to see Lily as the rest of the staff were seeing her—and Evie was right. She looked...strained. Just how much was her mother's behaviour weighing on her?

He wanted to pick her up and take her home—only it was seven at night and she was about to start the night shift and he was about to go off duty. She was Lily the Independent, as was her right.

'How's it going?' he asked from the doorway, and Tom saw him and beamed, and Lily turned and smiled but her smile was much more contained.

'Brilliant,' Tom said. 'I can bend every single thing that needs bending. I'm fully weight bearing. I don't know why they won't let me home.'

'They won't let you home until they're sure you're strong enough not to fall,' Lily said severely. 'You go home early, you risk coming back in with a broken hip. Is that what you want?'

'No, but—'

'And Luke and I are caring for both farms like champions.'

'Have you cut down the dividing fence yet?' Tom demanded.

Lily smiled but her smile was forced. 'You guys haven't cut down the dividing fence in the whole time Luke's owned his farm,' she said. 'I don't see why I should make a difference. Luke, is it okay if we have a birthday party for Tom in your apartment next Saturday?'

'A birthday party...'

She fixed him with a look that would have withered stronger men. 'Tom turns seventy-five on Saturday, and he's due to go home on Sunday. He's made so many friends here we need to do something to celebrate. We can't do it in the ward so I thought we could have a bash at your place. We could invite anyone from here who's grown fond of him. Maybe we could invite Patty and the boys from the farm.'

'They won't want to come,' Tom said, startled.

'We'll never know until we ask,' she said serenely. 'Pete's Bar does catering. I checked and he said no problems—and Ginnie says they do awesome cakes. I'll get balloons and—'

'Hey,' Tom said, starting to sound uneasy. 'How many people?'

'I don't think,' Luke said carefully, 'that Tom's ever celebrated a birthday in his life.'

'Why not?' She looked astounded. 'Why ever not?'

Because they'd never thought about it, Luke thought. Tom had grown up in the same sterile environment he had. His parents and grandparents didn't notice birthdays. After Luke had come to Australia, Tom had occasionally given him gifts, things he'd noticed he might like. They'd been awesome gifts; Checkers to start with, a trail-bike, an amazing sound system, furniture for his student digs at university. None of those gifts had been for his birthday.

He'd known when Tom's was, though. Once, when he was in his early twenties, he'd made an effort, brought a card and a cake and a bottle of whisky and gone back to the farm for it.

'Should'a rung before you come,' Tom had said. 'I'm clearing blackberries from the back paddock today. Could use a hand, though.'

He'd ignored the birthday card. They'd eaten the cake without lighting the candle, and he'd put the whisky away for later.

'Birthdays are fool nonsense,' Tom said now, and Lily glared.

'I like fool nonsense. I can't believe you've passed seventy-five birthdays without being forced to blow candles out. Right, you have a week's notice to develop some lung power. Seventy-five candles is huge.'

'Just you and Luke,' Tom said, belligerent.

'*And* your friends.'

'I don't have friends.'

'If you don't have friends I'll eat my hat,' she declared. 'Let's see what happens.'

'Are you out of your mind?' Outside in the corridor Luke let fly. 'Of all the stupid… Tom's been a loner all his life. What sort of a statement is that—*If you don't have any friends I'll eat my hat.*'

'The statement of someone who knows he has friends,' she said evenly. 'And the statement of someone who knows he needs them. If you're going to stay aloof for the rest of his life, the more people he has around him the better.'

'He wants me to stay aloof. He trained me in the art.'

'No,' she said flatly. 'His parents trained him and your parents trained you. I'm seeing two guys who haven't got the courage to decide what they want for themselves.'

'At least we've figured where we stand. Not like you, letting your mother get away with making outrageous demands.'

'As your parents' training makes outrageous demands on you,' she snapped.

'Then you crack first,' he said. 'Call the bank and reclaim your money.'

'Go in and hug your uncle,' she said. 'No? I rest my case.'

'He doesn't want—'

'Doesn't he?'

'A birthday party...' He raked his hair. 'Honestly, Lily, no one will come.'

'Patty's coming.'

'You've already asked her?'

'She's bringing lamingtons. I know I should have asked first, but it'll be fun. How are you at blowing up balloons?'

'I wouldn't know.'

'You're about to find out. Now I need to find Elaine. She says her Graham makes fantastic piñatas. You think Tom would like one in the shape of a horse?'

'This is not a kid's party,' he snapped.

'No,' she said, thoughtfully. 'But if it's the first birthday party Tom's ever had it needs to be a good one. I think it'd be best if we both stay here on Friday and Saturday night—or at least I'll need to stay. There'll be stuff to organise. Patty will take care of the animals for us, then we can both take him home on Sunday. He'd like that.'

'This is all about what Tom wants.'

'Of course,' she said, meeting his gaze head on. 'What else would it be about?'

'Lily…'

'Dr Williams!' Cathy, the lady who delivered ward meals, was heading toward them with her trolley. 'This party on Saturday…'

'You didn't,' Luke said, and Lily shrugged.

'This is the Harbour. I hardly needed to spread the word myself.'

'I'm so happy it's happening.' Cathy was beaming. 'Your Uncle Tom's lovely—and when he's out of hospital he says I can take my little boy up to see his horses.'

'He said that?' Luke felt winded.

'So of course we'll come,' Cathy told him. 'I make great fairy cakes, with red jelly and cream. Would you like me to bring some?'

'Yes, please.' Lily said, beaming back at her. 'Can you make lots? I have a feeling we're going to need them.'

'A birthday party. In your apartment.' To say Finn was hornswoggled was an understatement. 'I assume you're not expecting me to come.'

'Not if you don't like piñatas, lamingtons and fairy cakes,' Luke said.

'I don't.' Finn surveyed his friend with care. 'You're letting them get to you.'

'Them?'

'Women.'

'No,' he said but he was. One woman.

'You're not sleeping with her,' Finn said, and it wasn't a question.

He sighed. Finn the omnipotent. 'Enough with the commentary.'

'But you're nuts about her.'

He thought of Lily as he'd just seen her, beaming, excited, happily making Tom happy. There was only one way to answer Finn's question. 'Yes.'

'You going to tell Papa what's wrong?'

'I suspect Papa wouldn't be interested. Besides, you won't tell me about your arm.'

'It's getting better, whereas you and Lily… You're playing some game.'

'We're not.'

'She's only contracted here until the end of the week. Then she leaves?'

That brought him up with a jolt. After the party she'd be gone?

That's the plan, he thought, and said so.

'I see,' Finn said and Luke thought he did see. Far more than he wanted. 'Then it's back to normal?'

'I hope so,' he said, thinking he wasn't hoping anything of the sort. He should be—but he wasn't.

'Whisky's a cold bedmate.'

'Yeah,' Luke said, and suddenly he'd had enough of this conversation. 'You'd know,' he said savagely and walked away.

'I love a party!' Ginnie was practically squeaking with excitement. To give her her due, Ginnie had taken it upon herself to visit Tom every afternoon while he was in hospital. Lily wasn't sure how much Tom appreciated her visits, but Ginnie chatted and Tom let her, and they seemed to have formed a sort-of bond. So of course she needed to be invited. She was delighted, but she had reservations. 'But your apartment's so dreary. Can I decorate?'

'Of course,' Lily said, thinking, Hmm... Luke seemed to like grey.

'Jungle theme,' Ginnie said decisively. 'What sort of cake are you getting? No, don't worry about it, you have enough to sort. I'll talk to Pete. And I'll tell the guys to sort the drinks.'

'The guys?'

'The boys from the chopper rescue will be coming,' Ginnie said, as if it was a given. 'And the physios, and the nurses from Tom's ward. Ooh, it's just as well you have a big balcony. How many are coming from the farm?'

'I'm not sure.'

'Don't worry, we can cope, no matter how many.' Ginnie waved an airy hand. 'I'll haul Teo in. He's head of paediatrics, you must have met him. He's only met Tom once—I dragged him in to visit last week—but if there's a party there's Teo. I bet he can persuade his aunts to do some cooking. Do you think Tom would like his aunts?'

'I have no idea,' Lily said faintly.

'This hospital is so good at parties,' Ginnie declared. 'Saving lives and giving parties.' She giggled. 'It's a great mix. I couldn't bear to live anywhere else. I've never really thought that Luke liked being part of it, though. Isn't it lucky he finally has you to drag him into it?'

* * *

Friday was huge. Luke's operating list was long already and two emergency cases stretched him to the limit. It was nine before he had finished.

He wasn't going back to the farm. Lily would be in his apartment. Despite his fatigue it felt okay. More, it felt good. He headed back to Kirribilli, opened the apartment door—and was met by a jungle. Ferns, foliage and jungle growth was everywhere. Green netting, pith helmets, spears were hanging from the ceiling. A hulking plaster tiger was about to pounce from behind the settee.

He stood, stunned.

'It's from Kipling,' Lily said happily from under a mountain of green balloons on the floor. 'Do you like it?'

'Kipling?' he managed.

'*Jungle Book* was Tom's very favourite childhood book,' she said. 'I asked him when I was looking for a theme. Ginnie's been helping. Do you think we've succeeded?'

'Yes,' he said, trying to get his breath back. His lovely cool apartment. A jungle.

'You want to blow up balloons? Ginnie says we need to hang them in the foyer and on the letter-boxes downstairs. Elaine was helping but Graham rang to say he knows where he can get a gorilla suit. They've gone to find it.'

'Great,' he said, and sat on the floor and started blowing up balloons. He couldn't think what else to do.

'You needn't look like that,' she said.

'Like what?'

'Like your life's been taken over. It's one party. Tom will be back at his farm next week, I'll be gone and you can get right back to your nice solitary self.'

'I've given up on my nice solitary self,' he said. He blew up two balloons while he watched her blow up four. He thought about what he needed to say. What he should say. What he had to say. 'Did you know you're beautiful?'

'So are you,' she said, and she put down the balloon she was blowing and met his gaze, direct and true. She smiled. 'Luke, I'll sleep with you tonight if you want.'

If he wanted…

There was a statement to take a man's breath away.

'My mother rang,' she said, dropping her gaze, tying string to her balloon. 'She found me. She must have rung every hospital in the country. Admin has this apartment as my address so she rang here. She was almost hysterical. I've told her I'll be home on Monday.'

'No,' he said, and it was a gut reaction.

'I don't have a choice,' she said, only a faint tremor

in her voice betraying emotion. 'But I've been think-ing. I'd really like to sleep with you before I go. It just seems...wrong not to. In so many ways we seem so...perfect.'

'We are right.' It was practically an explosion.

'No,' she said, and sighed. 'Sadly we're not. We have two insurmountable obstacles, my mother and your crazy idea that I need protection. But if they didn't exist... I'd really, really like to sleep with you. That is, if you'd like to sleep with me. Would you?'

And how was a man to answer that? He looked across at her, in her faded jeans and sweatshirt, her tumbled hair, her mountains of balloons.

She looked back at him, calm and sure, and there was no need for an answer.

Balloons were forgotten. Party organisation was forgotten.

Everything was forgotten but this woman. He kissed her and then he rose and tugged her up with him. He kissed her again, long and deeply—and then he lifted her and carried her to his bed.

She woke and sunbeams were drifting over her nose. She was spooned into the curve of Luke's body. He was holding her as if she was the most precious thing in the world.

She'd never felt so alive, so wonderful, so loved, in her entire life.

The cramps had subsided. Where was stress now? She felt amazing.

She didn't want to move.

Any minute now she must. She had a party to organise. Guests were arriving at midday. Balloons still needed blowing up.

She wasn't stirring for balloons. She wasn't stirring for anything.

This was an illusion, she thought, and then she thought this whole month had been an illusion. Pretending they were a couple.

The night hadn't been an illusion. The night had been mind-blowingly, wondrously perfect.

The alarm went beside the bed. She'd set it last night when she was moving her gear into the bedroom.

Before Luke had come home.

Home. It was where she felt right now. Her perfect place.

'You're not a dream.' He was awake, his hold on her tightening. 'Whose idea was it to set the alarm?'

'It'll stop ringing in a minute,' she whispered. 'If we ignore it.'

Like the world might not intrude. If they ignored it.

'What has to be done?' he asked, and she out-

lined her list, her body not losing contact with his
for a moment. Skin against skin, spooned against
the man she loved.

She'd asked him to take her to his bed and she
didn't regret it for a moment. Yes, she had to leave,
but for this last weekend…not to make love with
him…she would have regretted it for the rest of her
life.

Now she was only sorry she hadn't relented three
weeks ago.

Tomorrow she'd told Tom she'd go with him back
to the farm. Then she'd return to Lighthouse Cove.
But for now…

For now Luke was going through her items, one
by one.

'Balloons?' he said, kissing the back of her neck.
'First guests here get to blow up ten apiece. There's
nothing worse than standing around as an early guest
with nothing to do. Sausage rolls? I'll get Teo to
come early; we'll tackle them as a team. Hoovering?
Why on earth would we hoover when the place will
be covered with people?' He reached over and the
alarm was firmly turned off and then she was even
more firmly taken back into his arms.

'So what shall we do with all our spare time?' he
asked, and he kissed her nose, her hair, her mouth.
'Oh, wait, I can think of something. It's a big job,

it'll take two of us to complete, but it's totally essential. It involves me telling you how much I love you and you listening. And then there's a demonstration. So do I have your permission to swap your list for mine?'

She smiled. She held him close, she felt him kiss her, hold her, take her.

This had no future, she thought. There was only now.

For now, though, who could think of a future?

There was only Luke, and there was only now.

They showered and dressed—very hurriedly—just in time to let Teo in for sausage-roll making. Luke was heading over to the hospital to do a fast ward round and collect Tom. Lily was trying to remember a mental list that seemed to have vaporised.

Luke kissed her goodbye, which didn't help at all.

'You're not leaving,' he growled into her ear. 'You're my woman.'

My woman. The words hung.

'I think I'm a feminist,' she said cautiously, as Teo whistled loudly in the kitchen and pounded out pastry.

'It works both ways,' he said. 'I'm your man. We'll work it out,' he said, and kissed her again, and then he really had to go.

She set out glasses and plates and tied balloons into bunches. She moved onto the sausage-roll assembly line. Teo joked and chatted and she joined in, but her thoughts weren't on the party.

You're my woman. Possession. Worry.

*We'll work it out.*

How?

It wasn't possible. Last night had been a farewell gesture, she thought, pure indulgence.

There might be one more night, but then it was over.

From the moment Luke escorted Tom into the apartment and assorted guests shouted, 'Happy Birthday,' the party was a success. Tom's face said it all.

The first to greet him were his dogs. Patty had brought them from the farm, cleaned, brushed and wearing ribbons with balloons attached. They'd been subdued when Patty had brought them into this strange environment but one sniff of Tom, who they hadn't seen for weeks, had them unsubdued. Luke had had to hang onto Tom or he'd have ended on his back under their weight.

Luke steered him to a chair and when Tom stopped laughing and emerged from under the dogs he could see who was there.

The place was packed. There were hospital people,

the people he'd got to know in the last few weeks, Luke's friends.

There was Patty, who he'd expected.

There were more.

Almost every farmer within a 'cooee' of Tarrawalla was here. People he waved to over the fence, kids he saw getting on and off school buses, the local stock and station agent, the guy who sold him hay...

Patty had done the rounds, letting people know, and almost always the response had been the same.

'Tom Williams... Why didn't you let us know he was in hospital? Of course we'll come; what can we bring?'

In his own quiet way, Tom was beloved, Lily thought, watching people crowd round him, watching his eyes fill with tears. His neighbours had simply been waiting for permission to show it.

They were showing it now.

Luke put his arm around her waist and held her close.

'This is some gift,' he murmured. 'I would never have thought of it, but it's a miracle. How did you know he'd like it?'

'How many people really choose loneliness?' she asked softly. 'You and Tom had loneliness thrust upon you.' She smiled across at Tom, loving his reaction, loving the feel of Luke holding her even more. Even if it was transient, she was loving it. 'Tom told me about your childhood,' she said. 'It sucks. I thought mine was bad, but your loneliness must have been so much worse.'

'Yeah, but it's long past.'

'It's not past. It's holding you still,' she said. 'And it will until you get perspective. There's loneliness, there's crowding and there's friendship. The third doesn't necessarily mean the second.' She took a deep breath, deliberately lightening. 'Enough introspection. There's work to be done. I need to take more sausage rolls from the oven and you need to make a speech.'

'A speech.'

'Absolutely,' she said. 'Teo says you're good.'

'I would have liked some warning.'

'I'm giving you warning,' she said. 'Right after the smashing of the piñata, ready or not.'

He tried to figure out a speech. He moved among the crowd in his apartment, enjoying the buzz. He marvelled at Tom's happiness.

He watched Lily.

She was wearing a simple crimson dress and crimson sandals. Her curls were brushed and shining. She smiled and smiled.

He'd asked her to move in with him. She'd refused even that, but now he wanted more.

Somehow he had to persuade this woman to marry him.

For that to happen…

First, there was the obstacle of her mother. Second, he had to figure how to relax. How to let her be her own woman. How not to watch her every moment.

He knew why she'd refused when he'd asked her to live with him. He could see it; the anxiety he'd learned from Hannah would stifle her. But how to get past it? She was seeing that he couldn't—that there was no use pretending.

He would learn, he told himself. He must.

But first…her mother.

He'd never met her but he'd imagined her.

He didn't have to imagine her much longer.

They'd just finished smashing the piñata on the balcony. Sweets were scattering over the rail and down to the street below and kids were wondering whether they could reach street level in time to retrieve them when the doorbell went.

Luke was closest. He opened the door—and there was a woman. And a vicar.

He didn't need to ask who they were. Some things spoke for themselves. The man was in his fifties, flaccid, weak faced, wearing a religious collar. The woman was a diminutive version of Lily.

She was tiny, with shiny, jet-black curls, exquisite make-up—and not very exquisite clothes. Clothes that said *Look at me* in the worst possible way.

The plastic surgeon in him noted the lines around her neck, the skin on the back of her hands, age signals impossible to hide. He also noted the flawless complexion, nary a wrinkle, and he looked for—and found—the tiny scars under her ears.

She was sixtyish, he thought, but she was aiming for thirty. Good cosmetic surgery.

I bet Lily paid for it, he guessed grimly as the woman walked in, towing her vicar behind her.

'I'm Gloria Ellis,' the woman said brusquely to the room at large, her gaze darting everywhere. 'They said at the hospital that my daughter's here.' Luke turned to Lily, and Lily's face had blanched white.

'Mum.'

'Lily.' Gloria dropped the vicar's hand and headed for her daughter. 'Of all the selfish…! Do you know how long it's taken me to find you?'

'You rang yesterday,' Lily said dully. The sounds of the party were fading around them as everyone realised who this was. Rumours of this woman had swept the hospital and probably beyond. Everyone knew Lily's mother was trouble. The whole room was listening. 'I said I'd come home on Monday.'

'Yes, but the thing is that Lighthouse Cove is ghastly,' Gloria told her, ignoring the people around them, focused only on her own need. 'The things people are saying… Harold and I decided it's impossible to stay there a minute longer, and we can't get to Paris as we planned. So we need a nice place to stay. The girl on the switchboard at the hospital said this is a nice place.'

She took time then to gaze approvingly out of the windows to the harbour beyond, and she gave a decisive nod as if the thing was decided. She took Harold's hand again and faced Lily. 'It was wrong of you to run away,' she said severely. 'You knew I'd be worried. However, I've decided to forgive you and rather than you coming back to Lighthouse Cove we'll stay here with you. This looks much more fun.'

She smiled then, a cat-got-the-cream smile that turned Luke's stomach. 'So you're having a party.' Her smile encompassed the whole room. 'Are you all Lily's friends? I look like her sister, but I'm really her mother. I know, it's unbelievable but I was a child bride.'

She giggled.

No one giggled back.

The Harbour might be Sydney Scandal Central,

Luke thought, but the team was a close-knit community. It protected its own.

As did Tarrawalla. Lily had been living in Tom's
house for only a few weeks, but she'd been seen as
Tom's family and therefore she belonged.

Consequently she had two communities who were
looking at Gloria with outright mistrust. They were
moving imperceptibly toward Lily. Their body lan-
guage spoke of protection.

Gloria was beaming at Teo now, a full-on beam
which made Luke see exactly what Lily contended
with. Gloria thought she was a sex goddess, as simple as that. She was wearing a tight-fitting, leather
dress, which pushed her cleavage to impossible lim-
its, stiletto heels and fishnet stockings. She beamed
and pouted all at once, and even though she stood
beside the vicar, her eyes were darting from male
to male, and her invitation was obvious.

This was the woman Lily had promised to protect, Luke thought, feeling ill. He thought of Lily as
a child, a twelve-year-old, being asked to commit
her life to the impossible.

He thought of all the things he wanted to say to
Lily's mother. He glanced at Lily and he thought,
Not here. Not now.

Lily had wanted to be anonymous, he thought,
and now he knew why. That's why she'd come

here. She'd embraced—and been embraced by—
the Harbour community, she'd abandoned her anonymity, but things needed to be said now without
an audience.

'Let's take this to the foyer,' he said in a voice that
brooked no argument. 'Now. Ginnie, make sure the
door's shut behind us.'

'Sure,' Ginnie said, and suddenly Gloria and her
vicar found themselves propelled outside. Luke
towed Lily out after them, and Ginnie closed the
door behind them.

Lily was so white. He put his arm around her
waist but she was rigid in his hold. She was help-
less against a promise made when she'd been twelve.

Enough. If Lily couldn't say it, he'd say it for her.

'Gloria, Lily's promised to care for you,' he said
into the deepening silence, and Gloria's seductive
smile turned onto him straight away. She'd seemed
stunned when he'd ushered her outside but she was
making a good recovery.

'Yes, she did,' she agreed. 'She's a good girl, my
Lily.'

'But did you know,' he said, and his voice took on
a ruthless edge because ruthless was how he was
feeling, 'that a promise made under duress is not
legally binding? Neither is a promise made by a
minor. A minor, Gloria. That would be someone

under the age of eighteen. Lily made her promise when she was twelve. The way I see it, Lily's promise to care for you was made to reassure her father, who was under such pressure that he killed himself. If that's not duress, I don't know what is. And she was twelve. She was six years under the age when a promise is valid.'

'Luke, don't,' Lily said, distressed. 'Go back to the party. This is my business.'

'No,' Luke said. 'It might not be my business but I care, and because I care I need to speak the truth. Lily, this is line-in-the-sand time. You should have this out with your mother, right here, right now. You're sixty years old,' Luke said to Gloria. 'How can you still live your life dependent on the promise of a child?'

'I am not sixty years old,' Gloria snapped, aghast. 'How can you...?'

For answer Luke flicked her dyed black curls from her face, exposing the scars of myriad past cosmetic surgeries. He wasn't in the mood for games.

'I'm a plastic surgeon,' he said. 'Sixty? I was being generous. I'm thinking older.'

'How dare you?' It was a scream of outrage. 'What gives you the right?'

'I have the right because I love your daughter,' he said, 'and Lily needs to see you as you really are.

Lily also needs to see her promise for what it really is. It's unjust and unreasonable and she shouldn't be bound by it for a moment longer. She's cared for you almost all her life but it's time it stopped.' He turned to the vicar. 'You love this woman?'

'Y-yes,' Harold said, but he sounded doubtful. 'But Gloria needs her daughter.'

'Nonsense,' Luke said bracingly. 'How can one grown woman need more than you? And, Lily…are you saying that your father would have seen your mother settled with a man of the church, and not said you've done your duty and more? That you've fulfilled his promise over and over, and now it's time you stopped? It is time you stopped, love. Right now.'

'What are you suggesting?' Lily looked aghast.

'That you let your mother go,' he said, his voice softening. 'Not completely. I know you won't do that. But I also know you own the apartment in Lighthouse Cove—that somehow against the odds you've bought it and managed to pay for it. But it's in your name and your name only. So what I suggest is that your mother takes Harold back there, that you give her permission to live in your house, that you're happy to chat to her once a week or so on the phone but that's it. That's your twelve-year-old's promise fulfilled with honour, and with a lot more courage than your father ever could have expected of you.'

And then, as Gloria stared at him, speechless, as Lily stared back, white-faced, he took her hand.

'Tell her, Lily,' he said. 'Your dad did his best for your mother but he reached his limit and he couldn't take any more. Think about your dad right now. You loved him and he loved you. If he's looking down now he's seeing his ex-wife with another man. He's seeing his daughter who's been robbed blind. He'll be thinking...what will he be thinking, Lily? What would he be asking that you say right now? And more. What do you want to say?'

She looked at him and he met her gaze, pure and strong. You can do this, his gaze said.

She must.

And finally, finally, she did.

'Luke's right,' she whispered, and then her voice firmed. 'No. I should say that louder. Enough, Mum. I've done enough for you and more. Yes, you're my mother, but we're both grown women with independent lives. Go home to Lighthouse Cove with your vicar.'

'You have to come home.' Gloria was suddenly as ashen as her daughter. 'You can't leave me.'

'You have Harold,' Lily said, her voice growing more sure by the moment. Luke linked his hand with

hers and she held on, but she didn't need it. He knew
she didn't need it. The strength was there.

'You have Harold and whoever else replaces him,'
she said. 'But I'm not there as a stopgap any more.'
She glanced at the unfortunate Harold. 'Harold
seems nice. Solid. What about holding onto him?'

'You're expecting us to go home?' Gloria's voice
was a screech of outrage. 'We can't. How can you
expect us to? Besides,' she added and there was triumph in the outrage, 'we flew here on one-way tickets. And we don't have enough money to get home.'

*What have you done with my money?*' Lily closed
her eyes, but then opened them and shook her head,
as if shaking off a nightmare. 'No. It doesn't matter.
It's past. Mum, when I was twelve I promised Dad
I'd look after you. Dad was so distressed... All I
wanted was to fix it and I would have promised him
anything. But I can't fix it. He couldn't and neither
can I. But that's it. I don't know how you're getting
back to Lighthouse Cove but it's not my problem.'

Luke tugged her tight against him and she let herself be tugged.

'There's no need for you to feel bad,' he said, holding her close. 'Your mum's not on her own. She has
her vicar.'

'And help from me.' It was Finn—of course it
was Finn—appearing without notice from the eleva-

tor. 'My secretary's buying one-way tickets back to Adelaide as we speak,' he said jovially. 'Don't thank me, Luke,' he said, expansively. 'This is a birthday party, isn't it? Don't all guests bring presents? If not, we'll call it an early wedding gift.'

He turned to Gloria and the full force of Finn Kennedy power focused on her and her alone. 'Mrs Ellis, I have a hospital car waiting outside to take you to the airport. Lily, give your mother birthday cake to go, and two balloons—it'd be sad if the Harbour was seen as less than generous. Luke, escort your future mother-in-law to the car to make sure she's properly gone. Right, I need a whisky. Enough. Are you intending to let me into this party or not?'

Finn escorted her back into the party while Luke took her mother to the car. To her amazement there was no buzz of gossip; no one talking behind her back. The room sort of closed in around her. She had approval and warmth and support. She was hugged by people she hardly knew.

So much for being anonymous. Why had she ever wished for it?

'Good girl,' Finn said, gripping her hand. 'One problem fixed. Now fix Luke.'

'So what about you, sir?' she asked, wondering at her temerity. She'd seen him wince as she'd taken his hand, and she'd heard the talk. 'Rumour is you have a problem you won't do anything about.'

'Nothing that this won't cure,' he snapped, motioning to his whisky, but then he shrugged and smiled. 'And we can't fix everything in one day.'

Luke returned. 'She's gone,' he said.

Lily felt... Actually she didn't know how she felt. Weightless? Happy?

Free.

Luke hugged her and she hugged him back and she thought...she thought...

That he needed to make a speech. And that this was only part one of a two-part problem.

But as Finn had said, *'We can't fix everything in one day.'*


Tom returned to his ward, exhausted but happy, looking forward to a long sleep to celebrate his last night at the Harbour. The birthday party went on without him.

Luke's colleagues weren't abandoning this excuse to celebrate Luke's long-awaited inclusion into their social network. Hints failed. Threats failed. It was two a.m. before the last giggling partygoer staggered towards the elevators.

'That was some party.' Lily turned and looked at the carnage of the living room. 'This is some mess.'

'You want to clean up now or go to bed?' Luke said into her hair, and she thought about it. For about a nanosecond.

'Bed. But, Luke...'

'Mmm?'

'Thank you,' she said softly. 'I should have done that so many years ago. It seemed impossible. For you to make me see...'

'Think nothing of it, my lady,' he said, sweeping her into his arms. 'Have I asked you to marry me lately?'

'No,' she said, her heart seeming to skip a beat. 'I don't believe you have.'

'I don't have a ring,' he said, settling her on his bed with care. 'But hypothetically...' He kissed her long and deeply, and lowered himself onto the bed beside her. 'If I was to go down on bended knee with a crimson box...'

'I'd probably giggle.'

'And then say yes?'

'I'd say I'd think about it,' she said, trying to make herself think when he was doing truly delicious things with his tongue; with his fingers. 'And I can't think about it at two in the morning surrounded by chaos.'

'I can't see any chaos,' he said, searching for the zip to her dress. 'I can only see you.'

'That's a problem as well,' she said, and she tugged him close and held him tight. 'How can I think about anything when all I see is you?'

# CHAPTER TWELVE

SUNDAY they were due to take Tom back to his farm. Home.

They planned to collect Tom at ten and take him in Luke's car, with Lily following behind.

'We need a bigger car,' Luke said as they woke, and Lily stirred in his arms and thought she didn't need anything at all.

But... A bigger car?

'A family car?' she ventured, feeling like she was on the edge of a precipice. A warm and delicious precipice.

But... 'No,' Luke said, revolted. 'But something like John's SUV. If I'm to cart uncles and women around the countryside...'

Keep it light... 'Buy a roof rack, then,' she suggested. 'It's cheaper. And one of those luggage pack things. Tom and I can pack down small.'

'Ridiculous,' he said, kissing her nose. 'Lily, will you stay at the Harbour? You have a permanent job here any time you want. We could try living together.'

'You mean before you think of giving me that little crimson box?'

'I mean before you accept it,' he said. 'The crimson box is metaphorically on the table already.'

'That's a very big word for the day after the night before.' She snuggled into his arms and felt delicious. 'I guess...' She thought about it. 'Tom has an attic room with a huge cast-iron bed. Maybe we could set up there,' she suggested.

He frowned. 'Live with Tom, you mean?'

'He'll need us.'

'I guess...for a week or so.'

'A week or so.' She stilled. 'Luke, he needs you.'

'Not permanently. We'd drive him nuts if we shared a house.'

'You're very sure.'

'I'm like him.'

She stilled. 'Would I drive you nuts if I shared a house?'

'No!'

'I might,' she said. 'I hog the bathroom. My mother calls me a selfish cow.'

'Your mother's gone,' he said, kissing her. 'We have each other. We'll do what we need to do for Tom, and then we can come back here.'

'And leave Tom?'

'Not while he's unsafe, but after that... We'll install a housekeeper. Someone. We're loners, Tom and I. This is huge for me, loving you.'

'I should be grateful?'

'No, but—'

'Luke, Tom isn't like my mother,' she whispered. 'We love Tom because he's special, like I love you because you're special. You shouldn't love me because you think I can fit into a niche in your life, leaving the rest undisturbed.'

'Lily—'

'No,' she said, closing her eyes for a second, coming to a decision. 'You've made me see the problems in my life but I don't know how to do the same for you. But until you do… All I know is that you need to leave that crimson box in the undecided basket.' She took a deep breath. Regrouped. 'Right. Let's get Tom home and settled. I'll take on another month at the Harbour…'

'Not night duty.'

'Okay, not night duty.' She glowered at him. 'Is that because you want to be with me or you'll worry about me when you're not with me?'

'Both,' he admitted.

'We do need time,' she said softly, and she tugged him back into her arms. 'I shouldn't stay. I know I shouldn't. I see this whole black chasm where hope should be. Oh, but, Luke…'

'I do love you,' he said, strong and sure, and she kissed him and held him tight.

'I'm figuring that out,' she said. 'I just need to know what it means to be loved that much.'

They made love. They dressed and headed to Tom's ward with Lily feeling more confused than she'd ever been in her life.

Things felt so right, yet there was a niggle of doubt that wouldn't disappear.

Love without conditions… That was the dream, she thought, but Luke's love seemed to be conditional. On her being safe. On him keeping her safe. On him keeping his boundaries with Tom. On him keeping his own boundaries.

Maybe I need to change, she thought. He won't.

Still…she thought back to where she'd been four weeks ago and she wondered why on earth she was worrying. She'd met Luke and she'd fallen in love. Luke had rescued her in true heroic style. He was, quite simply, the most gorgeous guy she'd ever met. He wanted to marry her.

She should be over the moon.

A niggle…

The cramps were back again. That was another niggle.

Tom. She put niggles aside and greeted Tom with

smiles. They gathered his belongings. With Luke on one side and Lily on the other Tom walked slowly out to the doctors' car park and almost half the Harbour's staff wished him well on the way.

But they weren't leaving yet. They'd just reached Luke's car when Evie came flying out the emergency entrance.

Walk, don't run. It was a medical mantra.

*Evie was running.*

'Sit in the car,' Lily told Tom, and Tom sank gratefully into the passenger seat, unaware of impending problems.

'Luke…' Evie called. She looked…scared. 'Thank God I caught you. Can you come?'

'What's happening?' Luke was already striding to meet her.

'Road trauma,' she said. 'Four guys, all needing Theatre. I had to call Finn in as back-up. He was to cope with a ruptured spleen. He started—but he's just downed tools.'

'Downed tools…'

'His hand's shaking, Luke. Carl's doing the anaesthetic—he's got the guy under but Finn's backed from the table. Carl said he tried to pick up forceps but his hand shook and he put them down again. Luke, it's Sunday morning and there's no other surgeon who can step in. If you come now we can keep this under wraps, we can get a good result, but if you can't, we need to transfer him now.'

Lily saw Luke's shock.

A ruptured spleen…a patient already anaesthetised…

And it was road trauma. There'd be other injuries as well, she thought. Even though Luke was trained in plastics, he'd have been thoroughly trained in general surgery. He could deal with whatever had to be dealt with.

'It's okay,' she told him. She fished in her pocket and handed him her car keys. 'Tom's in your car now and it's much more comfortable than mine. I'll take him out to the farm. You bring my car later. Just get on and do what you need to do.'

Luke turned and faced her, looking torn. 'If anything happens…'

'What will happen?' she demanded. 'Don't you trust me with Tom?'

'Yes, but—'

'Then stop with the hang-ups and go fix a spleen,' she snapped, and held her hand out for his car keys. 'Go.'

'Yay,' she said as she turned Luke's little car out of the car park. 'Hooray for us. We have a sports car and the open road. Do you want to put the hood down?'

'We might get dust in our eyes,' Tom said dryly. 'Luke'd have our guts for garters.'

'He is a worry wart,' she said cautiously.

'He is,' Tom agreed. 'He drove me nuts when he first came to the farm. Used to watch me all the time. I know it was because he didn't have anyone else, but it drove me crazy. I kept telling him to clear off.'

Which wouldn't have helped at all, Lily thought. What ten-year-old Luke had needed had been a hug, but Tom had never learned hugs either.

'And then that wife of his died,' Tom said. 'It was like his worst fears were realised. I tried...you know...to get close a bit, but he wasn't having any of it. But you, lass...he's letting you near.'

'Maybe too near,' she said. 'I kind of like the freedom to get dust in my eyes when I feel like it.'

'Then we put the hood down,' he said.

'Let's live dangerously,' she said, and they did.

She wasn't enjoying it much, though. Her stomach hurt.

By the time he finished surgery it was almost dusk. One ruptured spleen plus the rest, he thought wearily. He'd finished with his guy, then assisted Brian with another.

He was exhausted.

Evie turned up as he dumped his gear and turned to leave.

'Sorry,' she said. 'I had no choice but to call on you.'

'I know. How's Finn?'

'Angry. He says he thinks he's torn a ligament and he's taking time off. He's not talking about it.'

'I'll talk to him.'

'You won't get any further than I did.'

Torn ligament? He didn't believe it for a moment. What to do about his friend?

He looked at Evie and she looked steadily back and he thought, She cares as much as I do.

The Harbour. A whole network of carers.

It was a shock, he thought, and what came next was more of one.

'And what's wrong with Lily?' Evie asked. 'Luke, is she pregnant?'

Pregnant. The word hit him like a slap.

'No,' he said, and then, more cautiously as he thought of the night before, 'I don't think so.'

'Why is she losing weight? That dress she was wearing last night was a size too big.'

Was it? He'd thought she looked gorgeous. But if Evie said so...

'Blood test,' she said. 'Insisting with Finn's impossible. With Lily at least you have some control.'

'Do I?'

'I imagine you do,' she said. 'I'd imagine Lily would have the sense to know her health's important. Are you going up there now?'

'To the farm? Yes.' And then he paused. His phone was ringing. He flipped it open.

The call was from Lily.

'I thought you should know before the Harbour grapevine tells you,' she said, and he could tell she was speaking through gritted teeth. 'I've just rung the chopper for an airlift. I know it's dramatic but I'm not facing those winding roads again in an ambulance. Luke, I've got rebound. I'm thinking my appendix has burst. I'm on my way in.'

'Lily—'

'Don't you dare panic,' she told him. 'I'm in control, we're managing nicely and if you panic I'll panic. I'm safe and I'm in control. Deal with it. And, Luke...'

'Love...' It was a hoarse whisper.

'Tell me you love me.'

'I love you,' he said, with all his heart.

\* \* \*

She woke and the pain had stopped and Luke was holding her hand.

She felt peaceful and warm and safe.

*Luke was holding her hand.*

'Did I die?' she asked cautiously.

'No.' The growl made her smile. Luke's voice was so-o-o sexy.

'Someone took my appendix out?'

'Brian Lassiter. Evie assisted.'

'I thought you might,' she whispered. 'But I'm glad you didn't.'

'So how long,' he said through gritted teeth, 'have you been harbouring a grumbling appendix?'

'I suspect months,' she said, and he almost groaned.

'Of all the stupid—'

'Hey,' she said. 'Don't call me stupid. How was I to know? I've been having rumbling tummy cramps, nothing major. My doctor back at Lighthouse Cove thought they were caused by stress, and how could I argue with that? Then I had what we all thought was gastro. I saw Marnie Chrysler and she thought I might have picked up a bowel infection. She gave me anti—'

'You saw Marnie?' Marnie did the family medical stuff in Outpatients. 'When?'

'Two weeks ago. I'm not stupid, and neither's

Marnie,' she retorted. 'An appendix is easy to miss, so you can stop looking like it's anyone's fault. It seemed to be settling—until today. I was feeling a bit odd on the way up the mountain. By the time I reached the farm I thought I was relapsing with gastro. Tom put me to bed and then I rang Patty.'

'Tom put you... And then you rang Patty...'

'I was ill,' she said evenly. 'Why wouldn't I? Anyway, Patty came over to help. I couldn't keep anything down. Patty's Bill had just decided he'd drive me back here when I started feeling rebound.'

Rebound. It was an almost sure sign of ruptured appendix. If you pressed on the appendix site, there'd be little extra pain as you pressed down, but excruciating pain when you released the pressure.

That she'd coped...that she'd recognised it...

'Patty and Tom already had things in hand,' she said. 'When I said rebound we thought ambulance and then I thought of the chopper guys and got greedy. Jack was at the party—he was on my speed dial.'

'You didn't think to ring me first?'

'Your phone,' she said with remarkable asperity from someone who'd just come out of anaesthetic, 'was on message bank. The thought of leaving things till you'd finished was unappealing. And I rang you second. So here I am.' She smiled weakly.

'And Brian's fixed me. At least, I assumed he's fixed me. I assume I no longer have an appendix.'

'No,' he said grimly. 'You don't.'

'Then you can stop looking like that,' she said. 'If I'm happy, you should be happy. You can't think how good it feels to finally know what was wrong. It's been a worry, having cramps for all that time.'

'You should have told me!'

'And had you worry as well? I had it covered, Dr Williams. I did everything I could. If you're going to feel guilty that I and my doctor didn't pick up on the appendix then you can go put your head in a bucket.'

And then her voice faltered. She was weaker than she was letting on, he thought. He looked down into her eyes and they were moistening.

She was feeling anger, he thought. She was distressed.

'Don't do this,' she whispered. 'I'm not wearing your guilt. If you think that my appendix is down to you then your ego's more massive than every surgeon I've ever met. I don't depend on you, Luke Williams. I'm me, and if you don't let me be me then I don't want anything to do with you. Period.'

And finally, finally, she started to cry.

All this… All she'd gone through, and now she started to cry.

He'd let her down.

And then he thought…

He *had* let her down, but it wasn't because he hadn't diagnosed her appendicitis. He'd let her down because he hadn't reacted as he should have reacted.

It was like waking from a nightmare. Walking from darkness to light. He looked down at the woman he loved with all his heart and he knew what he had to do.

He knew that he could do it. It was line-in-the-sand time. Right here. Right now.

With love comes trust. And faith.

And joy.

He wiped away her tears, and then, very carefully, very tenderly, he gathered her into his arms.

'Lily, I'm sorry,' he said, holding her close. 'I am so, so sorry. Can we start again?'

'Wh-why would we want to?'

'Because there're things I need to say,' he whispered. 'I need to say how much I love you. I need to say how proud I am of you, how much I love that you did what you needed to do with courage and plain good sense.'

'Luke—'

'Hush,' he told her, kissing her hair. Kissing her eyelids. Tasting the salt of her tears. 'Lily, I'm ashamed of myself that my first reaction was that it was my fault; and that my second was anger that you hadn't referred everything to me. I need to know—and I do know—that I'm in love with a woman who knows how to stand on her own two feet. I know you're the woman I love most in the entire world, and I wouldn't change you for anything. I need to hold you, but I also need to let you go.'

She sniffed. She sniffed again into his shoulder and she wound her arms around his neck and held.

'Ouch,' she said.

'You push this button for pain,' he said, withdrawing in an instant and showing her the plunger for self-administering morphine. 'One push and the pain will subside.'

'Codswallop,' she said weakly.

'Codswallop?'

'Codswallop,' she repeated, and she held him tighter still. 'No drug's giving me what I want. If you want to be a really, really effective doctor, Dr Williams, you need to kiss me now, because absolutely nothing else is going to solve my problems.'

'I love you,' he said.

'That'll do nicely,' she whispered, pushing her plunger because a girl had to be sensible. If she was to hold him as tightly as she intended holding him, she needed to be very sensible. 'For a start.'

* * *

Spring was the very best time for a wedding. Everyone said so, from the Harbour janitors to Erich the medical director himself. The weather forecast was watched with anxiety by practically the entire hospital, because practically the entire hospital was on the guest list.

'It's like Christmas.' Evie chuckled. 'We're trying to get every patient home because the staff has better things to do than play doctors and nurses.'

Of course the hospital couldn't be emptied entirely and some staff needed to be left behind. For them, the IT guys organised a video link, so the wedding could be seen in every ward in the hospital.

The linking cameras were set up by a rippling creek on a beautiful little homestead at Tarrawalla, just underneath Tom's house—on the farm they intended staying on for the rest of their lives.

Ginnie was chief wedding planner. This was a job after her own heart. Teo planned the feast afterwards; his aunts cooked their hearts out. Half the district cooked their heart out. The rest… Ginnie had them hanging heart-shaped lanterns from every tree, stringing streamers, setting out chairs, tables, sunshades, candles that doubled as mosquito repellent—no mosquito was going to get within half a mile of this ceremony, Ginnie decreed, and who was to argue with Ginnie?

Finn was best man. He'd gone on leave, and his arm seemed better. There were still problems, Luke thought, but even taking leave had been a big concession. Evie still worried about him.

Evie could do the worrying, Luke decided. He'd stopped worrying. It was forbidden in Lily's code.

He was especially forbidden to worry about Lily.

'If you worry about me, I'll worry about you,' she'd told him. 'You want my stomach to be tied in knots every time you leave home? No? Then cut it out with your own knot-tying.'

He had a handle on it. One appendix…one capable woman surrounded by an army of friends… He wasn't alone and worrying was stupid.

He had a wedding to focus on, and a bride. How could a man worry with that to look forward to?

Tom was giving the bride away. 'I know being given away by the groom's uncle is different,' Lily had told him. 'But my alternative's my mum or Harold and I'm not going there. I love Tom to bits and he loves me, so it's perfect.'

He did. Tom was surrounded, astonished, by the direction his life was taking. All these people… Friends… Family.

Luke's parents were there, trying to disapprove, trying to look superior. Ginnie had them in hand. Two champagne cocktails one after the other the moment they arrived, and they were already un-bending. There'd be no miracles, Luke thought, but he was pleased they were there.

And Gloria and Harold were there as well.

'You can come if you don't drink and you wear something respectable,' Lily had told her mother. 'Luke and I will pay for two nights at the Tarrawalla pub and for your air fares. No, you're not staying at the house, but we'd love you to join us for the day.'

Luke was pleased about that, too. Boundaries had been set, but Lily still felt she had her mother.

More, she had an entire family. A hospital and a farming community.

He was standing under the towering gums waiting for his bride. It was five minutes past the appointed hour. Where was she?

'Brides are always late,' Finn growled. 'They do it on purpose to put a man in his place.'

'Quoth the authority on weddings.'

'I've watched my share,' Finn said. They're like watching train wrecks—a man can't look away.'

'Finn...'

Finn gave a rueful chuckle. 'Okay, sorry. I know this isn't a train wreck. Even I, misogynist old bach-elor that I am, concede it's right for you. Lily has you wrapped round her little finger and you're going to love it.'

They went back to waiting. Ten minutes late. 'This is killing me,' he said.

About three hundred people were gathered round the clearing by the creek. Three hundred people were waiting for one slip of a girl.

For Lily.

'I'm guessing this is her,' Finn said, grinning at his friend as the music from Teo's mate's band overrode the sound of the kookaburras in the trees overhead. 'I'm guessing. I'm not sure an orchestra would play a wedding march for the arrival of a door-to-door salesman.'

Luke had already turned to see.

The outdoor seating was separated into two sections, with an aisle between for the bride to approach. He could see her now. She was coming down the hill from the house, Tom by her side.

Tom was looking dapper in a suit he'd bought specially—'I'm not hiring any suit for our Lily's wedding,' he'd told them.

He was on Zelda.

Lily was riding Glenfiddich.

The onlookers gasped as one, and so did Luke.

She was…exquisite.

Her dress was simple, white damask silk, with tiny capped sleeves and a sweetheart neckline. Her curls were loose and free. She was wearing simple diamond drops in her ears—Luke's wedding gift—and no other jewellery. She needed no other jewellery.

Woman and horse. The combination was more than breathtaking.

She was using a sidesaddle. Her gown clung to her breasts and waist and then flared out in a lovely sweeping skirt that draped over Glenfiddich's glossy black flanks.

Glenfiddich was looking like butter wouldn't melt in his mouth. If ever a horse could be said to be proud, it was Glenfiddich. Zelda trotted beside him and her eyes gleamed as well. They tossed their heads and practically pranced. These were horses on parade and loving it.

Once upon a time, Luke thought, seeing this woman on this horse had filled him with dread. Now he knew his Lily. She hadn't told him she was doing this but he knew her way with horses. She smiled at him as she neared and he smiled back, and his heart swelled with pride. His gorgeous, courageous, independent bride was on her way to marry him, and she could travel any way she liked.

The horses halted where the seating began. Luke started forward, involuntarily, to lift Lily down, but Finn took his arm and held.

'This is Tom's role,' he said, and it was. His uncle

lifted Lily down from her horse as if he were thirty-five instead of seventy-five.

Then he tucked her hand into his arm, and proudly walked Lily to her husband-to-be.

The music swelled and died.

Lily reached him, smiled at Tom, released Tom's hand and tucked her hand into his instead. She smiled and he smiled.

'Hi,' she said.

'You're… There are no words to describe you.'

She chuckled and loved him with her eyes. 'Try.'

'I love you,' he said, simply and surely, and her eyes misted with tears.

'That'll do for now,' she whispered as they turned together to commence their wedding vows.

'Come to think of it,' she added as he held her tighter. 'That'll do for ever.'

\* \* \* \* \*

# Mills & Boon® Large Print Medical

## September

| | |
|---|---|
| FALLING FOR THE SHEIKH SHE SHOULDN'T | Fiona McArthur |
| DR CINDERELLA'S MIDNIGHT FLING | Kate Hardy |
| BROUGHT TOGETHER BY BABY | Margaret McDonagh |
| ONE MONTH TO BECOME A MUM | Louisa George |
| SYDNEY HARBOUR HOSPITAL: LUCA'S BAD GIRL | Amy Andrews |
| THE FIREBRAND WHO UNLOCKED HIS HEART | Anne Fraser |

## October

| | |
|---|---|
| GEORGIE'S BIG GREEK WEDDING? | Emily Forbes |
| THE NURSE'S NOT-SO-SECRET SCANDAL | Wendy S. Marcus |
| DR RIGHT ALL ALONG | Joanna Neil |
| SUMMER WITH A FRENCH SURGEON | Margaret Barker |
| SYDNEY HARBOUR HOSPITAL: TOM'S REDEMPTION | Fiona Lowe |
| DOCTOR ON HER DOORSTEP | Annie Claydon |

## November

| | |
|---|---|
| SYDNEY HARBOUR HOSPITAL: LEXI'S SECRET | Melanie Milburne |
| WEST WING TO MATERNITY WING! | Scarlet Wilson |
| DIAMOND RING FOR THE ICE QUEEN | Lucy Clark |
| NO.1 DAD IN TEXAS | Dianne Drake |
| THE DANGERS OF DATING YOUR BOSS | Sue MacKay |
| THE DOCTOR, HIS DAUGHTER AND ME | Leonie Knight |

# Mills & Boon® Large Print Medical

## December

| | |
|---|---|
| SYDNEY HARBOUR HOSPITAL: BELLA'S WISHLIST | Emily Forbes |
| DOCTOR'S MILE-HIGH FLING | Tina Beckett |
| HERS FOR ONE NIGHT ONLY? | Carol Marinelli |
| UNLOCKING THE SURGEON'S HEART | Jessica Matthews |
| MARRIAGE MIRACLE IN SWALLOWBROOK | Abigail Gordon |
| CELEBRITY IN BRAXTON FALLS | Judy Campbell |

## January

| | |
|---|---|
| SYDNEY HARBOUR HOSPITAL: MARCO'S TEMPTATION | Fiona McArthur |
| WAKING UP WITH HIS RUNAWAY BRIDE | Louisa George |
| THE LEGENDARY PLAYBOY SURGEON | Alison Roberts |
| FALLING FOR HER IMPOSSIBLE BOSS | Alison Roberts |
| LETTING GO WITH DR RODRIGUEZ | Fiona Lowe |
| DR TALL, DARK...AND DANGEROUS? | Lynne Marshall |

## February

| | |
|---|---|
| SYDNEY HARBOUR HOSPITAL: AVA'S RE-AWAKENING | Carol Marinelli |
| HOW TO MEND A BROKEN HEART | Amy Andrews |
| FALLING FOR DR FEARLESS | Lucy Clark |
| THE NURSE HE SHOULDN'T NOTICE | Susan Carlisle |
| EVERY BOY'S DREAM DAD | Sue MacKay |
| RETURN OF THE REBEL SURGEON | Connie Cox |

| 1 | 2 | 3 | 4 | 5 | 6 | 7 | 8 | 9 | 10 |
|---|---|---|---|---|---|---|---|---|---|
| 11 | 12 | 13 | 14 | 15 | 16 | 17 | 18 | 19 | 20 |
| 21 | 22 | 23 | 24 | 25 | 26 | 27 | 28 | 29 | 30 |
| 31 | 32 | 33 | 34 | 35 | 36 | 37 | 38 | 39 | 40 |
| 41 | 42 | 43 | 44 | 45 | 46 | 47 | 48 | 49 | 50 |
| 51 | 52 | 53 | 54 | 55 | 56 | 57 | 58 | 59 | 60 |
| 61 | 62 | 63 | 64 | 65 | 66 | 67 | 68 | 69 | 70 |
| 71 | 72 | 73 | 74 | 75 | 76 | 77 | 78 | 79 | 80 |
| 81 | 82 | 83 | 84 | 85 | 86 | 87 | 88 | 89 | 90 |
| 91 | 92 | 93 | 94 | 95 | 96 | 97 | 98 | 99 | 100 |
| 101 | 102 | 103 | 104 | 105 | 106 | 107 | 108 | 109 | 110 |
| 111 | 112 | 113 | 114 | 115 | 116 | 117 | 118 | 119 | 120 |
| 121 | 122 | 123 | 124 | 125 | 126 | 127 | 128 | 129 | 130 |
| 131 | 132 | 133 | 134 | 135 | 136 | 137 | 138 | 139 | 140 |
| 141 | 142 | 143 | 144 | 145 | 146 | 147 | 148 | 149 | 150 |
| 151 | 152 | 153 | 154 | 155 | 156 | 157 | 158 | 159 | 160 |
| 161 | 162 | 163 | 164 | 165 | 166 | 167 | 168 | 169 | 170 |
| 171 | 172 | 173 | 174 | 175 | 176 | 177 | 178 | 179 | 180 |
| 181 | 182 | 183 | 184 | 185 | 186 | 187 | 188 | 189 | 190 |
| 191 | 192 | 193 | 194 | 195 | 196 | 197 | 198 | 199 | 200 |
| 201 | 202 | 203 | 204 | 205 | 206 | 207 | 208 | 209 | 210 |
| 211 | 212 | 213 | 214 | 215 | 216 | 217 | 218 | 219 | 220 |
| 221 | 222 | 223 | 224 | 225 | 226 | 227 | 228 | 229 | 230 |
| 231 | 232 | 233 | 234 | 235 | 236 | 237 | 238 | 239 | 240 |
| 241 | 242 | 243 | 244 | 245 | 246 | 247 | 248 | 249 | 250 |
| 251 | 252 | 253 | 254 | 255 | 256 | 257 | 258 | 259 | 260 |
| 261 | 262 | 263 | 264 | 265 | 266 | 267 | 268 | 269 | 270 |
| 271 | 272 | 273 | 274 | 275 | 276 | 277 | 278 | 279 | 280 |
| 281 | 282 | 283 | 284 | 285 | 286 | 287 | 288 | 289 | 290 |
| 291 | 292 | 293 | 294 | 295 | 296 | 297 | 298 | 299 | 300 |
| 301 | 302 | 303 | 304 | 305 | 306 | 307 | 308 | 309 | 310 |
| 311 | 312 | 313 | 314 | 315 | 316 | 317 | 318 | 319 | 320 |
| 321 | 322 | 323 | 324 | 325 | 326 | 327 | 328 | 329 | 330 |
| 331 | 332 | 333 | 334 | 335 | 336 | 337 | 338 | 339 | 340 |
| 341 | 342 | 343 | 344 | 345 | 346 | 347 | 348 | 349 | 350 |
| 351 | 352 | 353 | 354 | 355 | 356 | 357 | 358 | 359 | 360 |
| 361 | 362 | 363 | 364 | 365 | 366 | 367 | 368 | 369 | 370 |
| 371 | 372 | 373 | 374 | 375 | 376 | 377 | 378 | 379 | 380 |
| 381 | 382 | 383 | 384 | 385 | 386 | 387 | 388 | 389 | 390 |
| 391 | 392 | 393 | 394 | 395 | 396 | 397 | 398 | 399 | 400 |